AF450089

BLINDED

By Fransánchez

Translated by ZionXVI

<u>Warning</u>

Contains bloody and sex scenes

Fransánchez

Index

Fransánchez

Episode 1

The Computer Scientist

He emitted a desperate groan as he felt a sharp pain, opened his eyes and glimpsed someone dressed in white. His eyelids closed again and another painful prick forced him to wake up. The frenzy of staff in white dressing gowns and pajamas throughout the room was unceasing. That tide of activity that swept from one side to the other overtook him, he didn't know where he was or what was happening, he tried to get up, but his strength failed him, he chose to desist and return to Morpheus' world.

"What's your name, what's your name?" he listened insistently.

"Ra... pha..." he muttered with both eyes closed.

"How many pills did you take? How many pills did you take?" the young woman questioned again in a firm and determined voice.

He found it difficult to keep his eyes open, he just wanted to sleep, and those people were bothering him.

"Let me... I am... sleepy..."

"No way. Wake up!" he ordered the voice.

The pain caused by the heavy pressure on his earlobe opened his eyes, and he angrily searched for the cause of the attack, but his wrists were bound to the stretcher.

"Calm down, cooperate, it's for your own good."

He understood that he was in the hospital, in the emergency room, he was very sleepy, but alive. The last thing he remembered was the titanic effort he made to press the red emergency key on his state-of-the-art mobile phone.

Suddenly he was more lucid and alert; the intravenous injection given by the nurse on the young doctor's orders had had an immediate effect. The doctor, already in a softer tone, began to interrogate him for his medical history. She asked him if he had any allergies, if he had any illnesses, if he was taking any treatment, his family history. Rapha answered docilely while he was fascinated by the beauty of the doctor; "Alice", he could read off the identification card that was hanging from her unbuttoned gown.

For the first time in his life, he felt relaxed, calm and at ease with a woman, except for his mother of course. He entertained himself by watching Alice, her swaying around the room, writing on the computer, whispering orders to the nurses in a velvety northern accent:

"Activated charcoal stomach pump, then psychiatric consultation."

Rapha remained fascinated, Alice was tall and slender, brunette with tied long hair in a ponytail, blue eyes and full lips. Her swollen breasts were trying to escape from the generous neckline, wasp waist, behind the medical scrubs you could guess a tight ass.

"Yes, my shift today is twenty-four hours, I leave at eight in the morning," he heard her say to a fellow worker.

After the typical sermon about the goodness of life and the stupidity of suicide, she encouraged him to look for solutions to his problems. Alice said goodbye very politely and wiggling her way through the critical care room to the hallway to her office. She had to continue attending to the long line of patients who were still waiting for medical attention in the waiting room. Rapha watched her in a daze as she walked away.

After finishing vomiting, he was transferred to the psychiatric area. First thing in the morning he had no choice but to have a long and sincere talk with the specialist.

Rapha was a chubby kid, even in his own in style, not good at sports and all the games that required physical effort. Given his peculiar appearance, he often had problems at school and in his small hometown, famous for its iron bridge, which is located in the Alpujarra Mountains of Granada.

He was always the focus of ridicule and scorn from his classmates, who made fun of him. This caused him a great social isolation, becoming a reserved person. In his childhood he only found refuge in novels, comic books and history encyclopedias, becoming an avid devourer of literature of all genres.

He reached his adolescence suffering from extreme shyness. The only advantage was that he had a lot of free time to devote to study and to one of his favorite hobbies, computers.

Genetically he was more like his father than his mother, so he inherited his short, greasy hair and short height.

His move to the city and entry into the university environment did not change his life much. He already had premature alopecia and great myopia, adorned with thick, unstylish, high-prescription glasses that made his morphology stand out even more.

He graduated with excellent grades, which allowed him to easily look for his professional future as a programmer. He found it in Almería, a city in the southeast, on the Mediterranean coast. But too far away from the only stable and loving relationship of his whole life, his little family. He adapted his work to his lifestyle, became his own boss. His profession was carried out at home, with no schedule. He was presented with the development of an application or the design of a web page, he only had to concentrate, immerse himself in the task and dedicate all his time to it. He found that he worked better at night, his Internet connections were clearer, his computer was much faster, and his web pages went up more quickly. So, he changed his life habits, sleeping more in the morning and working on his projects in the afternoons and evenings.

One day he found himself in his forties, with no friends, no partner, no family, no relationships, just alone and bitter. Given the circumstances of his life, he always had a depressive personality that he solved with medication and many hours of work.

He liked sex a lot, like almost everyone else, although he had never had any relationships, he was a virgin and incapable of even talking about banal things with any woman. He was so nervous that he could hardly speak, causing a ridiculous stutter. On one occasion, newly arrived in the city, he tried to hire the professional services of a prostitute. When he went up to the room in the boarding house, while the girl was undressing, he felt so nervous that a bitter taste in his mouth made him retch, which he could not suppress, without warning and without being able to avoid it, he threw up on the prostitute. The girl, who had already been paid in advance, was furious and found the perfect excuse to finish her work and send him off with a shout:

"But that fatso will be disgusting! As my name is Susan, don't ever look for me again! Pig! Get the hell out!"

After the colossal brawl, Rapha, very ashamed, hurriedly fled from there in a pitiful state of anxiety. After this disastrous experience, his sexuality continued to be reduced to his collection of porn films and his very dear and faithful friend "masturbation". His life circumstances provoked a strong rejection to society, a resentment and a deep general hatred.

That fateful dawn, things were going terribly wrong. He was stuck, as if thick, he was not doing well at all. He decided to take a break, watch some TV. There was nothing interesting, lots of quiz shows, those very easy to answer, hooks to get money out of people over the phone. He found in a local TV channel a great and beautiful girl, with impressive curves. She was doing a strip tease to soft music, after five minutes he had an erection and after another five minutes the man was cleaning his semen with a handkerchief.

The unfortunate senior continued feeling bad, she went to the medicine cabinet to take her usual antidepressant pill but in a fit of tears he took the whole bottle. He lay down to wait on the couch, while watching on TV what he missed most, the soft and velvety human contact of a woman. Rapha found it increasingly difficult to hold the eyelids, they insisted on closing, he couldn't cope with them. He didn't know why, moved by an unconscious spring, perhaps the instinct of survival, he stretched out his arm trying to grab the mobile phone from the table, the cable that kept it plugged in to charge the battery prevented him from doing so and it fell to the floor on the other side. Rapha got up to pick it up, his legs no longer supported him and he also fell to the floor. After crawling, he managed to reach it, it was off, he turned it on with difficulty. He could not fix his eyes to mark the pin, he pressed the red emergency button and when he heard the voice of the operator, he only managed to sigh "help" before losing consciousness…

Rapha left the hospital convinced of the idiocy he had committed; the washing of the stomach had been an experience he did not want to repeat ever again. He had had a hard time convincing the psychiatrist that the autolytic crisis had ceased and that he would take things differently, facing the problems of his life.

He arrived home, but an unpleasant surprise awaited him, the door was smashed in, only kept closed by local police stickers that read "Do not cross". The interior was a bit messy, he was too tired to tidy up, he wanted to sleep, so he left the mess for later and blocked the door with a simple chair. He went to bed leaving his bedroom in the dark, with the blinds completely down and the opaque curtain extended, as was his custom. As he entered the dream, he couldn't help thinking of Alice who had made a deep impression on him, he knew she was unreachable, she would never notice a guy like him. He fell asleep whilst fantasizing how he could get that woman's attention.

He rested for several hours, although, despite being in a deep sleep, distant voices woke him up. He was drenched in sweat, hearing voices again, but this time closer. He opened the bedroom door and the voice was louder, he couldn't understand what's being said, but yes, it was here in his flat, he deduced that someone had snuck into the house taking advantage of the broken door.

"A burglar!" he thought worriedly.

He had some computer equipment worth more than fifteen thousand euros, he was going to find out about the "crook", he took a heavy lamp from the bedside table and went quietly to the kitchen where the noise was coming from. He entered and found the individual on his back, as he was not that brave, he wanted to avoid a confrontation, he didn't hesitate and gave him a strong blow on the head. The delinquent fell to the floor unconscious and a trickle of blood that flowed from his head, quickly invaded the kitchen floor. The sight of so much blood frightened him.

"I've killed him," he thought.

He knelt down and turned the body over, leaving it on its back.

"Shit, it's the neighbor!"

I didn't even know his name; I only knew him from "hello" and "goodbye" in the corridor. He took the thief's pulse and didn't find it, he wasn't breathing, and he was indeed dead.

He panicked and a thousand thoughts sprang to mind: the police, the arrest, the trial, the prison...

"Keep calm, Rapha," he thought aloud.

He could claim it was self-defense, that he was under the influence of strong medication, plus what the hell was he doing to the neighbor in his house, snooping around? But what if he wasn't dead, he wasn't a doctor. The best thing was to ask for help, so he picked up his cell phone and dialed 112, the line was busy. He tried again with 061, the line was busy, then he dialed 092, this one did give a call, although they didn't take it.

"What a shameful country," he thought.

He tried 091, a recording told him to call back after a few minutes. He decided to focus on 112 and dialed again, busy, he was pressing redial for a few minutes and nothing.

The man looked more closely at the neighbor, and from the pool of blood that had run through the kitchen and the increasing paleness of his face, he knew for sure that he had died. He decided to go down to the street to ask for help, and as soon as he left the doorway he ran into a man.

"Help me," he said.

His interlocutor replied in a bad mood:

"What, are you blind too? Another one with the little joke? Well, fuck you!"

And he walked away, tapping away from the sidewalk with his long white cane.

Rapha didn't understand anything, suddenly he noticed a strange commotion and when he paid attention, he noticed the landscape, it was dantesque. A multitude of vehicles had collided with each other, others had merged by great impacts, unrecognizable, some were smoking, others were burning, and others were embedded in the shops and commercial premises. A car from a well-known French manufacturer hung dangerously from the slope of an access ramp to an underground parking lot.

People were constantly asking for help and assistance. They moved clumsily and senselessly, stumbling over the untidy tangle of cars, twisted irons, vehicle parts and pieces, fenders, mirrors and torn doors, various scrap metal scattered on the asphalt.

Some people were engulfed in flames, others lay motionless on the ground, bloodied, and others skidded and fell comically into the roadway from the layer of oil and debris spilled by the wrecked cars. Others, frightened, remained inside the wrecked vehicles. Some pedestrians were huddled together, crowded around, forming a strange gathering, like a melee at a rugby match.

He was deeply impressed by a bus that had collided with one of the busiest stops, crushing and running over a large group of citizens, sowing the sidewalk of mutilated bodies in different formats, amputated limbs and viscera bathed in blood.

In another area of the street, he observed a woman fall down a flight of steps, remaining motionless on the ground. Another man was seen sinking into a construction ditch, another stumbled over a carpet of glass from a broken shop window, cutting his hands and arms several times. Suddenly a smoking vehicle exploded, knocking out the people around it and causing a deadly shower of scrap metal and debris that reached another group nearby.

He turned his head to look down the street and the scene was similar all over the avenue, with several fires causing a smoky fog.

Rapha was petrified by the surprise, what had happened, no matter how much he thought about it, he didn't know what was happening. Surprisingly someone collided with him and took him by the arm, with great anguish he begged and pleaded for help. Another stumbled behind him and grabbed him by the waist, crying out for help. A very close individual braced in the air and managed to grab him by the other wrist, while a boy of about seven years of age hugged his thigh, and almost in unison, in front, a mature lady of about fifty years of age hugged her neck tightly. Rapha was trapped, surrounded and while everyone was shouting, he tried to get away with it without success. He could not move, they were hurting him and he felt very overwhelmed, he tried to reason with them but they had entered into a kind of collective hysteria, everyone was talking at the same time making communication impossible. He couldn't stand it anymore, more people were coming, so he chose to lose his balance and throw himself to the ground dragging them all. He managed to get some of them to let go, where it was easier for him to get rid of the rest and roll a few meters. He got up quickly, sore and eroded, and turned the corner.

He was trying to get over the shock when suddenly someone collided with him again and grabbed his arm tightly while imploring and pleading for help. He recognized him right away, he was the manager of the supermarket on the ground floor of his building.

"What's the matter with you, neighbor? What happened?" he asked.

"I can't see, I can't see anything, there's no light, everything is dark, I can't open my eyes," he said.

"What do you mean you can't see, something has fallen inside you, some liquid or sand?" Rapha replied as he looked straight into his eyes.

His eyelids were closed and somewhat swollen, his eyelashes were like a welded together yellowish, viscous paste that oozed from his tears.

"No, the blinding light, the blinding light!" he repeated nonsensically.

Rapha still didn't understand anything and the man was saying incoherent things.

"What blinding light? Calm down and tell me everything so that I can help you," he said.

The manager calmed down a bit, told him how he was in his supermarket, saying goodbye to some customers, when suddenly everything turned white, a powerful light suddenly appeared and invaded everything for a few endless seconds. Then a great pain appeared in his eyes and from that moment he had lost his vision, he was blind, it was very difficult to open his eyes, even if he managed to open them, he still couldn't see anything. He also told him how he heard the brakes, the beeping of the vehicles, the collisions and the shouting. He asked him if he had asked for help, and he answered that he had, but no one had come.

It was extremely hot, unusual for that time of year, Rapha was still drenched in sweat and it was very difficult for him to think and make decisions. He let go of the manager's arm and headed down the street, while the manager shouted again for help. He kept walking, eluding and avoiding everyone in his path, he had learned his lesson.

As he passed a parked vehicle, he noticed that the driver was repeatedly trying to connect to emergencies on his "hands free", the lines were not working, that story sounded close to him. As he watched this scene, he deduced that no one would come to help, everyone would be calling the emergency lines, and what if the help services were the same and they had also lost their sight, what if there was no one to help them, what if he was alone to take care of everyone? There were so many people, how could he organize everything, what to do first, what decisions to make, he began to feel the weight of responsibility on his shoulders, he panicked and ran.

As he ran down the avenue aimlessly, the view of the adjacent streets was very similar: smoke, screams, disorder, chaos, junk, inert bodies, blood, and human clutter. Rapha stopped running immediately, his extra kilos and the suffocating heat prevented him from doing so. He was very thirsty, so he went to a nearby bar. But before he entered, a tearful old woman, with unusual speed and skill, grabbed his arm and asked for his help. Rapha looked at her in terror and without thinking, almost instinctively lied to her:

"Help me, I got blind!" shouted Rapha.

The old woman let him go, realizing that he was in the same situation as her, and that he would be of little use to her. Rapha, surprised by the ease with which she had solved the problem, entered the empty bar. There was a television connected, it only emitted an image of an empty table, without sound. He changed channels looking for information about what had happened, in some stations the programming was normal, films, series, documentaries. On others it was time for the news, but there was no news, in one they focused on the floor, in another you could see a room with people feeling up the walls, the panorama was comical to some extent.

He poured beer into a glass and drank several one while thinking. The man felt overwhelmed, overtaken by events, powerless, and was convinced that his help would be like a drop of water in the immense desert, that he could do little. He already had his own problems with the last night's events, and he felt resentment and hatred towards this society that had tripped him up so much during his life. He had always felt marginalized, humiliated, why would he help them now? He thought that perhaps now was his time, he was overcome by a certain sense of revenge. At that moment a young and beautiful girl entered the bar, groping and stroking the air. She was wearing slender thighs because of a very short miniskirt that flapped when she moved, leaving her buttocks naked with only a thong in between. Rapha got up and hesitated, the effects of alcohol clouded his reasoning, he remained pensive for a few long seconds. He approached her from behind with stealth, pushed her and imprisoned her tightly on a table, the surprised girl stirred with all her strength as she screamed with great desperation, he didn't care about the woman's screams, as they overlapped with those of the street. With his weight he prevented the girl's struggle and waited patiently, after a few minutes the girl's strength began to decline and with her defenses down, he took advantage of the situation and slipped clumsily inside her. After a few brief and strong swings, he relieved himself after many years of abstinence. The young woman only had strengths to cry, Rapha fastened his fly and invited her to sit down to rest, he gently grabbed her arm to guide her but the young woman drew strength from her own weakness, becoming agitated again in an attack of hysteria and feeling liberated, she ran away madly, tripping over chairs and tables until she finally collapsed on the floor, bruised and exhausted.

Rapha left the bar while turning his head in all directions to make himself sure that no one would have witnessed the events, leaving the poor girl there amidst pitiful sobs, thinking that her first time had been hideous and too fleeting.

The depraved man walked without remorse, convinced of the justification of his actions, of how badly society had behaved towards him, about morality or immorality, which he had to adapt to the new situation and if it favored him, he would take advantage. He owed nothing to anyone, it felt good to him, almost euphoric, sure of himself, he thought that his personal problems, inferiority complex, could be diluted by the unexpected turn of events. He had no obligation to help the community of which he never felt part. Besides, he was not a hero, nor a fireman, nor a policeman, nor a doctor... doctor! At that moment he remembered Alice, the intense, good and shocking impression she had made on him. She did deserve to be saved and helped, he was capable of making an effort, and he could be a hero…her hero, so he would find a way to get her attention.

Looking for an available car, Raphael found one with the keys in, and its radio was playing low volume. Perhaps it was broadcasting a news program, he tuned in to the stations, various programs were playing, probably from those pre-recorded programs, the announcer was asking for help on a channel because she had gone blind. He kept looking and on one got some vague news, the announcer, who had also lost his sight, but not his nerves, was repeatedly broadcasting some sort of emergency report. He told how most of the phone lines were overloaded with calls. That it all started with a powerful blinding light of which they were unaware of the causes. He ventured several hypotheses, it could be because of an atomic bomb, an unlikely possibility, and the country did not suffer direct threats or reasons for any aggression.

Nor was any new type of terrorist attack ruled out. Perhaps the entry of a large meteorite into the Earth's atmosphere would cause a large flare, another possibility was due to an unknown weather effect or some anomaly caused by the Sun such as a huge solar flare. The announcer continued to give some basic advice, to stay at home because it was the safest place, the one we knew best by heart, not to venture out into the street because it was dangerous and to wait for help.

"Ha! Help…" Rapha thought ironically.

He started the car and began to drive through the desolate street, it was impossible to move forward, having to avoid the other parked vehicles, since no one was driving. The worst thing was the people who were in the middle of the road and moved very slowly, when he managed to get a pedestrian to leave the path, on the other hand was again interposed another, it would take ages to reach the hospital. He had to find another means of transport, he found the possibility of running over people very excessive. He abandoned the car and walked for a while; the man was already beginning to adapt to the new situation by avoiding the area of action of those affected. He made as little noise as possible and, if he had no choice, Rapha would shout for help, just like the others.

He found a moped, he had never been skillful at driving them, although it might help. He drove clumsily to the hospital, and of course this vehicle was much more practical with which was easier to avoid people and vehicles.

He went into the emergency room, it was very much like the zombie movies he liked so much, chaos and disorder everywhere. Of course, the health staff was also affected, no one helped anyone, and everyone had enough to do. She wandered through the corridors, the rooms and the doctors' offices, she couldn't find her, where would she be, she suddenly remembered that last night Alice had told another colleague that she was leaving at eight in the morning, so she thought maybe she could be in the car park. He went there by bike but didn't find her. She looked around a bit, until she saw an area under construction with a sign that said STAFF PARKING, FORGIVE THE HARDSHIPS, WE ARE WORKING TO IMPROVE. He approached and suddenly saw her, she was sitting on a curb in the shade, with a big pair of sunglasses covering her eyes, someone was with her, and he assumed it was a companion.

"Hello, do you need help?" Rapha asked.

Alice stood up with a start, between frightened and surprised.

"Yes, yes, we've gone blind after the great glow, take us to the emergency room please, no one's been here for hours. We haven't dared to go ourselves because the area is full of holes and potholes from the work."

Rapha explained that he was on a motorbike and that they could only go one at a time. He helped Alice up, told her to hold on tight, and they set off while he noticed Alice's breasts placed on his back.

Rapha thought it was time to decide, he certainly was not going to the emergency room, why? There would be no one there to help. He decided to take her home and hide the fact that he had been her patient the night before. When she got off the bike, Alice, who was surprised, told him that it had taken too long to get to the emergency room. She asked what was happening, after hearing the cries for help from the people who were clumsily heading towards them, following the noise of the motorbike. He hastily informed her that they were not safe there and were in danger. Then he would explain everything to her more calmly because it was imperative to go out there, he implored her for a little confidence and after overcoming Alice's suspicions, he got her home.

He sat her down on the sofa, Alice asked for water, Rapha went to the kitchen to get a glass and surprise! The neighbor's cadaver was still there. Because of the frenetic succession of events, he had completely forgotten about it.

He felt sorry for him and lamented his bad luck, the killer understood that because of his blindness he had entered his flat by mistake. The remorse punished him because that situation could have been avoided if he had acted differently, if he had tried to scare him, if he had tried to dialogue… Of course, everything became clearer after that but there was no solution.

Rapha returned to the living room and after giving the glass of water, Alice asked for her colleague who was waiting in the hospital car park. Rapha, first of all, gave her a brief explanation of the current situation, where everyone had lost their sight, where no public service was working, and told her, with great exaggeration to horrify her that gangs of survivors were looting, pillaging and killing. He told her that because he was sleeping completely in the darkness when the phenomenon occurred, he got no affection. He suddenly got the idea that more people like her partner might not be blind. But the tricky man saved that problem for later.

He asked Alice to wait for him there, while he went to pick up her friend. He closed the door of the room for safety and so that she would not notice that he was taking the killed neighbor's body out. After dragging the heavy neighbor to the street, he placed him next to a wall.

Well, he had to start getting organized and setting priorities. He had to think about food, security, medicine, how lucky he was to have a doctor at home. He would solve any problems that arose by improvising as only he was good at.

He went into the supermarket under his house, where he met his neighbor, the manager. Under protest and a struggle, he took him out to the street, took away his keys, closed the doors and lowered the security shutters. The manager was left outside helpless, banging on the door and shouting.

"He'll get tired very soon," Rapha said.

He made a small inspection; the market was fully stocked with food and all sorts of products. All the freezers were working and replete of goods. It had a back door with independent access to the block's aisle, he could enter and leave the store comfortably without having to go outside.

While walking by the grocery store, he had an unexpected encounter, the supermarket assistant, a young blonde girl was lying in a corner. Rapha approached her stealthily and found that she was asleep. Rapha did not count on this setback. Now he would have to open the heavy metal blinds of the big door again to get her out of there or he could take her out through the back door and go out through the entrance of the block. He thought about it for a few moments as he watched her. The truth was that the young woman was attractive, she wore a short gown that left a smooth, soft thigh in the air, and her lips were fleshy and pink. He thought better about it and after a lewd smile, it occurred to him that her situation was ideal for satiating his base instincts repressed for years. Now was his moment and he was not going to waste it, his imagination evoked the pleasant instants of a sultan with his concubines, his particular harem. He felt powerful, strong, and euphoric and a surge of self-esteem encouraged him.

There was plenty of food there, he could feed her as well. Determined not to expel her he thought he could not leave her there, she would put his pantry at risk, and could spoil something, break it, or cause a fire by accident. He could lodge her in his house next to Alice, although he thought about it more carefully, perhaps later. Rapha had to think, consider, he came up with a brilliant idea, the house of his neighbor, who died "by accident", was the house next to his own, because of its proximity it was much more practical for such plans.

He needed those house's keys, so he went out the front door of the building, approached the body of his dead victim. He looked for the keys and when he found them, he went up to the flat which it was empty. Quickly he prepared it, tidied it up a bit, removed the elements dangerous for a blind one, and went down again to get the girl. She was still asleep, he had to make up a coherent story to get her to come up to the flat without any problem. He looked in the office and found a portable radio, he tuned in to the station he was listening to, there was still that announcer with his short piece of news, more exhausted, but there he continued. Rapha gently woke the girl, who after a few moments reacted sharply:

"I still can't see, I can't see anything, who are you, what happened?" the girl asked nervously.

"Calm down, my name is Rapha, I am a friend, listen to the radio for a moment and you will understand the situation."

The girl heard the news and fell silent in surprise. After a brief cry, she asked for her manager, Rapha told her he didn't know, that there was no one else there, but the girl heard the knocking on the door and asked for them. Rapha explained to her that they were gangs that wanted to enter the supermarket to rob it and that they had to leave from there since they were not sure. The girl nodded and they both went up to the neighbor's flat where he placed her as comfortable as possible.

Rapha gave her a long talk about the new situation, the world had changed and they had to survive. She was blind, weak and defenseless, unable to fend for herself. The outside had become dangerous, because of the gangs and because for her, now, the outside was a new and unknown world, with its architectural barriers and its difficulty to get food, medicine, welfare. He told her not to worry, that he would take care of her, feed help and protect her. For the time being, this would be her home, which she would have to memorize and learn the location of her belongings to be able to move around safely.

The girl was very grateful for the help, saying that she did not know how she could express her gratitude; Rapha took the opportunity and in a friendly tone, took the girl's hand and let her know that he was single. That he needed company, that he had needs, that she could become a great burden and a great responsibility, but he would make a great effort to comfort her. He bent over her and gave a kiss, but she was startled, turned around and walked away getting scared. She let him know going into shock confessed that did not like that situation, the girl begged the man to let her go and take her home.

Rapha was furious, he shouted at her that there would be no one in her house, or they would be blind or dead. What did she want, to be left all along right in the street, at the mercy of the troublemakers, sure that they would rape her among all of them and then kill her? Rapha told her that he had already seen many bodies lying in the street, and if this did not happen, she would die of hunger and thirst anyway. While she was sobbing the young girl made an ultimatum, what she perhaps needed was some time to consider and to learn what lay ahead of her being alone, without any help. He would lead her to experience a similar situation, suffering from hunger, thirst and need. He turned off the water and removed all the food and drinks which were found in the kitchen cabinets from the apartment. He slammed the door, turning the key so she couldn't get out.

He continued with his plan, he needed to secure his place, so he decided to go door to door to see if anyone was still alive there. In one of the houses, an overweight, frightened, mature woman opened the door, asking for help. Rapha reacted quickly and told her that he was from the ambulance service, which would take her to the hospital emergency room for treatment. The confident lady followed him, but before that Rapha asked her for the keys to her house to close the door and after putting them in his pocket, he lied to the lady indicating that he had put the keys in her bag. They went down to the street, he turned two corners, made her confuse a little and let go of her arm, stealthily leaving the woman there, while she, surprised, called out to him insistently.

During the short journey Rapha observed something curious, some people were beginning to pool themselves and form human chains that moved along the walls, not knowing very well where to go.

He returned to the block and resumed the inspection of the building. All the houses were empty, except the attic, where a young woman's voice asked from inside. Rapha answered that he was from the rescue services, the woman opened the door, being just as blind as the others. He looked at her carefully, she was young, tall, slender, and precious.

"This one for me collection," he thought, giving him the go-ahead.

Rapha gave her a brief explanation of the events according to his interests, explained that the authorities had assigned him that area and he was responsible for taking care of and attending to those affected. It was important for her safety to remain at home while the authorities finished setting up special camps with the minimum of services and guarantees. Rapha was again surprised by his capacity for imagination and improvisation. He cajoled her into giving him a copy of the key, checking the house and the pantry. He prepared her a cold sandwich with sliced bread, gave her some brief recommendations for her safety and promised to return the next day.

Rapha was tired, he had been busy the last days, full of experiences, emotions and strange situations. He had momentarily forgotten about Alice who was still in his house and with the door to the flat open, he hoped that she hadn't gone out to explore and that she would have been hurt. He found her on the sofa in the living room, sleeping like a log, tired from the many sleepless nights spent by her guards. He went over to look at her, her beautiful face was serene, her large breasts were rising and falling with the breath. She was beautiful, and, while caressing her cheek, Alice woke up startled. Rapha reassured her, but Alice asked him immediately about Anthony:

"Anthony, what Anthony?" Rapha answered, being surprised.

"The colleague who was with me in the hospital car park, if you had gone to pick him up," she asked.

Rapha had completely forgotten about that detail, he hesitated, he didn't know what to answer. He couldn't tell her that he didn't even intend to go and help him, he had to bust through a plan quickly. He would just tell her that I hadn't found him and he was gone. It wasn't a good idea; she could insist that she go back to look for him. It was in these thoughts, when Alice was sad and tears ran down her cheeks. Fortunately for Rapha, Alice interpreted that long silence with which something tragic had happened to her friend. Rapha, with a mischievous mind, thought he had found him dead inside a ditch, his head split open by a deadly blow. The girl's friend having been impatient for the wait, surely, he tried to reach the emergency room by his own means, reaching such ending tragically. They wailed for a while as he comforted her.

Rapha was hungry. He was an expert cook by which it was one of his favorite hobbies, cooked something fast for both, desserts, exchanged views on the new situation and what would be their best strategy as well. They decided that the best thing was to stay at home for a few days waiting, seeing how things developed outside, that Rapha would go out to bring food.

Alice told him that she needed some things from the pharmacy. She explained she suffered from irregular and painful menstrual periods, that to control them she took contraceptive pills and aspirins for general malaise. She also asked for a series of eye ointments and eye drops, some pills with unpronounceable names, gauze and anti-inflammatory drugs. She wanted to start taking medication and try to reverse her blindness. Rapha wrote down the order list and went in search of the pharmacy.

In the street many of the fires were mitigating their strength, although there were still some isolated ones, they were not dangerous because they could not spread. As he walked along the sidewalk, he seemed to spot two people turning a corner in the distance, too agile and determined to be blind. His skin was bristling, it would only be a matter of time before he met someone unaffected, in these circumstances this encounter could be somewhat dangerous. Rapha felt fear, he had never been of the brave gender.

Rapha was lost in thought when, by chance, he found a local police motorcycle lying on the ground. He looked around for the user of the motorcycle, found him a little further away, embedded in the side window of a vehicle, half a body inside and half a body outside, with his legs in the air. Of course, he was dead, but he still had his work belt, his standard-issue weapon, ammunition and handcuffs with their corresponding keys. Rapha gathered them and put everything in his rucksack.

Going into a pharmacy and gathering what he needed for Alice was not as easy as it seemed. The search was more effective due to element of surprise than anything else, as several shelves were located in the center and along the warehouse, surrounded by as many shelves leaning against its walls. All of them five levels high, all filled with boxes of medicines, finding what Alice needed among so many shelves were similar to finding a needle in a haystack. Rapha was taking too long and was about to give up when he discovered by chance that the medicine boxes were arranged in alphabetical order. He cursed himself for his clumsiness, and after a few slow minutes he finally completed the order.

Alice was desperate to get her long-awaited medicines. As soon as Rapha arrived, she was interested in the order, especially the ophthalmological ointments. Alice was sure that she could recover her vision, trusting in her wide knowledge of ophthalmology. She asked Rapha to read the ointment's instructions very slowly, especially the dosage. Alice told him to prepare some sterile gauze carefully and put some of each ointment in it, then she rubbed the conjunctiva of each eye gently. She was convinced that with the proper protection, visual rest and the effect of the pharmaceutical components could be recovered and improved.

Rapha left Alice lying with her eyes covered and went to visit the girl in the supermarket. When he opened the door, the floor was silent, nothing could be heard. The man went down the aisle with caution without being conscious what he would find and any situation was possible. The supermarket girl lying on the bed in the master bedroom was awake and with clear signs of having sobbed for a long time. She immediately informed Rapha that she was hungry and very thirsty, Rapha told her that she already knew what the price was and wanted to charge in advance, she answered him bathed in tears, that she was a virgin. Rapha did not soften and replied that someday it would have to be the first time.

"If you only knew that I'm almost a virgin too," he thought.

The girl continued crying and replied that she didn't like men either, she preferred women. Rapha was surprised by the confession; he didn't even expect it. He thought that perhaps it was a ploy, although he was indifferent to it, true or false, for his purposes this did not represent any impediment. Her sexual preferences meant nothing for him, anatomically she was a woman to perfectly fulfill his task. Rapha answered impatiently, he did not care and she would have to decide. The girl, in the midst of pouting, unbuttoned her robe, leaving her splendid body in underwear. Rapha quickly undressed and while he put a condom on his already erect penis, he promised to try to go carefully and delicately. Rapha also had his doubts, he only had a theoretical background based on the multitude of porn films he had consumed. He chose to lower his panties and spend a good time to warm up, it was difficult for him, but he succeeded. The girl started moaning and breathing heavily, until she emitted a series of muffled groans. He realized she was ready, so she stood on top of her, spread her thighs, slowly went inside, and after a few hip movements the senior pulled out.

They lay for a while next to each other, she remained silent, thoughtful, with her eyes absent, and she did not cry anymore, he commented with satisfaction that she had not done it bad.

"By the way, what is your name?" he asked in a kind and gentle tone.

"Elizabeth," she answered, "and I am hungry and thirsty".

Rapha, more cheerful and happy, prepared her some food. While Elizabeth gobbled up in despair, Rapha asked her if she was really a lesbian, she replied that there was a time when she had many doubts, but these were cleared up by a relationship with a classmate. He arranged the floor better, so that she was more comfortable and informed her that he would return later.

Rapha had to attend to his other girls, his work was piling up. He went up to visit the girl in the attic, rang the bell while he opened the door, here he didn't expect a hostile environment, for the moment.

"Hello, I'm from the rescue service!" he shouted.

"Yes, I'm in the living room, come in," she replied.

As Rapha went into the attic he looked more closely at the rooms. The attic was very large, with four bedrooms, a splendid terrace with exceptional views. It was decorated in great style, in luxury, and a lot of money had been invested there.

"You have been a long time coming back, I am hungry, I have only been able to eat some fruit since yesterday. Forgive my manners, we haven't introduced ourselves, my name is Susan."

They went to the kitchen and while Rapha was preparing something to eat, he began to test the ground for his interests. He wanted to do it without haste, tactfully, as he already had Elizabeth insured, he could wait a little longer with this one, to manipulate her even more. He explained to her that outside things were not going well, that there were many gangs looting and catching, there were rapes. The authorities were not controlling the situation and the special camps for those affected were going to be delayed. I had a lot of work to do, I had to take care of many people, especially the elderly ones. In addition, few people were able to see and they were finding more and more blind people, so he had no choice but to visit the woman not so often. Unless there was a more personal reason to visit her more often and give her more favorable treatment, Rapha insinuated with special intonation. Susan remained silent for a few long seconds, then smiled and left Rapha puzzled by the response he received. There was no problem that she would do what was necessary to be as well attended as possible, that she would treat him so well that she would not want to leave. Then that stunning woman got up awkwardly, looked for him in the kitchen and stood there, leaning on the counter, pulling down his pants and kneeling down began to perform fellatio with great skill. Rapha was in paradise, although he had unloaded a while ago, it was so much scarcity that he had suffered for years, that he did not care. He immediately responded to the stimuli produced by Susan's sensual and soft lips, and after a few long minutes, he thought that the truth the woman was hungry, because she swallowed it all.

After the aperitif, Susan continued tasting the lunch prepared by Rapha while she told him her biography. She worked as a high-class prostitute, visited luxury hotels, and went as an escort to business trips and various events. She was doing very well and earning a lot of money, so she could afford a penthouse like that in the center of the city. She also confessed that she did not dislike her job too much, even allowing herself to have the liberty of not accepting orders if the client was not to her liking. She had always been very liberal and a bit of a nymphomaniac, which is said to be a woman open to all kinds of experiences. She would do everything necessary to keep Rapha in touch with her. The woman was helpless and defenseless, her current goal was to survive and if she had to do it by going over the top, she would. Rapha thought he had won the lottery, that he had been lucky, Susan was the opposite of Elizabeth, active, complacent and expert, highly-qualified. He decided to be half honest with her, explained that the situation was worse than she imagined. That there were no authorities, that no camp was being set up and that he was not from the rescue services, but someone who wanted to take advantage of the situation. He saw the positive side of things, he did not have to attend to any area, he was going to keep a close eye on her, as long as they kept the agreement. He needed intimate company and she needed care and food. Susan agreed, although she wanted to polish up details of this verbal contract later on. Especially in the areas of personal hygiene, contraception and sexually transmitted diseases, as these were subjects that she followed very closely because of her work.

Rapha remembered Alice, it was his turn to visit her, and he began to think that it was a nuisance to be every moment visiting the girls. It consumed him three times as much effort, the situation was exhausting and impractical, he spent all day cooking individual menus from here to there. In addition, the girls also stayed a lot of time alone, he decided that the ideal was to unify them all in a house and that great attic was ideal, perfect for its great size and amplitude. He told Susan that he had more friends on other floors and that he thought it would be a good idea to bring them to the attic. He could make food for everyone at once, he would not have to divide her time and they could keep each other company. Susan agreed as long as they respected the privacy of her bedroom and the bathroom attached to it. He decided first to go up to Elizabeth, he told Susan his story with Elizabeth, how he met her, how he approached her and how he forced the girl to have sex. Susan told him that she would talk to her and help as much as she could to ease the situation, but asked him not to tell what she did for a living, since most people prejudged her badly about it.

Rapha quickly went down to get Elizabeth, meekly allowing herself to be moved to the attic. She loved to have company and more so if it was a female one. He placed her in one of the rooms and gave her a tour of the attic, so that she was able to familiarize with the rooms, the furniture and the distances, in short, so that she could memorize it. Rapha went home, leaving the two girls chatting as friends.

Rapha found Alice lying on the bed, bored of waiting so long. She was happy to hear him, as she was afraid that something had happened to her. Rapha explained to her that he had been very busy, saving two other girls, one in the supermarket and the other in the building, in the attic. The most convenient thing for everyone was to move there, it was much more spacious, the two girls were already there waiting for them. The idea seemed very good to him so they moved to the attic. Rapha made the respective introductions, while he prepared some tapas for dinner. The girls narrated their experiences with the phenomenon and exchanged impressions of their last days. It seems that Susan and Elizabeth had had an existentialist talk since there was a more relaxed and relaxed atmosphere and when Elizabeth narrated how they met she omitted the lurid details of the relationship, perhaps also due to the famous Stockholm syndrome she already suffered from.

Alice indicated to Rapha that he should return urgently to look for another pharmacy and to collect many more medications since now there were three that needed ointments and other elements to try to improve their visual ailments. Rapha said he agreed, although they could not see how he frowned and his countenance became more serious and worried.

After dinner everyone retired to their respective rooms to rest and Rapha took the opportunity to sneak into Susan's bedroom:

"I feel like it now," Rapha demanded.

Susan nodded, asked him to lie down on the bed. She massaged him for a while, put a prophylactic on him and climbed on top of him, introduced it with skill and started to ride slowly, progressively increasing the rhythm, while Rapha massaged her big breasts with delight. She increased the volume and cadences of her moans until she reached a great orgasm. Rapha could not stand the excitement any longer and after some ridiculous spasms he felt an unspeakable pleasant sensation. Susan lay down on the bed, Rapha tried to kiss her on the mouth, but Susan stopped him, kisses on the mouth, no, that was not part of the deal, she only kissed for love.

"It's 300 euros for the service," joked Susan to relax the tension of the moment.

"Are you going to charge me, if you enjoyed it too," he replied being surprised.

Susan laughed and explained that her orgasm had been a fake. While she was working, it was rare that she had an orgasm, the woman almost always pretended, it was a technique to excite the client and make the coitus shorter. In fact, the prostitute told him that she calculated getting rid of her current client in less than six minutes. Rapha was a little upset, now was not going to be very demanding, but later wanted something more elaborated. Susan told him not to worry, that she was a professional and very skillful, besides she was going to play a little bit with Elizabeth, train her, prepare her and convince her so that in a few days they would be ready to give him a trio. A trio! Rapha loved the proposal a lot, he was impatient for that moment to come and in the following days every time he thought about it some sticky drops would stain his shorts.

He got up at early morning, it was almost dawn, the street lighting was working poorly, but enough to wander around. Some lampposts were lit, others were not, and others had fallen to the ground due to collisions.

The pharmacy was on the main avenue, so he went to it, he was surprised that there were few blind people wandering the streets.

"They must have taken refuge wherever they could," Rapha thought aloud, "they must have made the motto 'every man for himself'

Although when he reached the avenue, something did not sit right with him, something had changed there. Before, the avenue was collapsed by vehicles, now it was too, but in a different way, someone had moved cars, so that they had left enough space to circulate on it. There was no longer any doubt, more people had been saved from the solar flare, it was the most logical cause that Rapha found to explain what had happened. Anyone who was not exposed to sunlight would have been saved from blindness, people who slept at night during the day, or people who at that moment were in basements or rooms without windows to the outside. The fact is that this was the confirmation of his fears, he already knew that he was not alone and had left his gun at home, he hesitated to come back for it or take a chance and continue. He kept going, there was the pharmacy, and it was open and deserted. He began to compile the order list, he collected the eye ointments, more boxes of pills with names that were very difficult to remember, this time he didn't take so long, he had learned the alphabetic lesson. When he saw some beauty creams, he put them in his rucksack, thinking that the girls would like them, because of the coquetry. He looked for the contraceptives and carried several boxes,

"For several months," Rapha considered.

Next door were the boxes of condoms, he decided to take quite a few, as he was beginning to make longer-term plans and did not count on getting anyone pregnant. He thought that raising children almost on his own would mean taking on more responsibility, although later he did not rule it out because of the issue of repopulating the planet, in case the phenomenon was worldwide and the majority of the planet's population was blind, perhaps we should bring in healthy children. I was thinking about this when, without waiting, two men entered the pharmacy and found themselves face to face. After the initial surprise, Rapha noticed that they were not armed and that relieved him a little.

"Are you all right, I mean if you can see," asked one of them in surprise.

"Yes, of course I can see well, I'm not blind, are you?" Rapha replied, as he scanned the sunglasses they were wearing.

They answered that they were not blind. They introduced themselves, the one with the singing voice was called Frank, and they told him that they had managed to gather a fairly large group of unaffected people and that they were organizing to help most of the blind people. They were gathering them in the Sports Pavilion, had managed to put out most of the major fires and had also managed to clear some of the vehicles on the main avenue. Although there was a lot of work to be done, all those people had to be fed, they could not leave the bodies out in the open for long, and to avoid epidemics and disease, they had to be disposed of. They suggested that he join them, who needed all the help they could get, the more the better. They felt that they could not wait for the government's help, as the problem seemed to affect the whole country. Rapha didn't like the idea, that is, the guy suggested that he go with him to work as an undertaker, or as a cook and a waiter. Was he crazy or what? He was managing very well on his own and had better prospects.

"All right," he said, "are you in the Sports Hall, I've got a group of blind people safe and sound, I'm looking after them. I'll get them, I'll get our belongings and we'll meet there in an hour or two, we'll have to watch out for the bands."

"Gangs? What gangs?" asked Frank strangely.

Rapha explained that he had seen a small group of people, he couldn't say how many, robbing shops, making fun of blind people and even making fun of a girl. He sensed that she had been raped, since he heard her scream hysterically. He thought about helping her but he found it very dangerous and risky so he chose to flee the place fearing for his life. Frank answered, that they had not seen anything, although it was better to know the news. They would take more precautions, they complained about the evil of the human being, that how could people be like that. Rapha nodded to them, while laughing to himself.

"See you later," Rapha said.

As he thought quietly, "goodbye suckers" he went away in the opposite direction to the attic, taking a long detour and looking back from time to time, in case they had been followed, to throw them off. Better not to trust anyone, because he would continue his plan according to his own interests.

When he arrived, he picked up some rubble from the ground and threw it with all his strength on the big plastic sign screwed to the wall of the building.

The lettering of SUPERMARKET was shattered and scattered on the floor making it unreadable. Then he got into a big van from the surrounding area and drove it up to the sidewalk. He managed to block the entrance of the shop and in turn blocked this van with two others similar. From the street it was already very difficult to access the supermarket, in fact it had been so disguised that if you did not know it was impossible to know it was there.

As he went upstairs, the girls were already up and talking, but Alice changed the subject, she asked Rapha about the medicines. As a good health professional, her faith in his knowledge and commitment did not make her lose hope in recovering the vision. She reminded Rapha how the gauze was prepared with the ointments, and then an ocular occlusion was performed on each of the girls' eyes. Rapha obeyed Alice's orders, prepared six eye patches and smeared them. He soaked the patches with cream, but with cream from the beauty products he had also brought, hiding the bottles of eye ointments and eye drops. He had thought about it and since that medication could help them recover their vision, it was something that went against their interests. He needed this relationship of dependence to satisfy her carnal instincts and feed her self-esteem. The girls were somewhat grotesque with the patches and somewhat annoyed, complaining of a slight itchiness in the eyes, Rapha suggested that it would be the ointment taking effect, anyway did not think that beauty creams hurt them more than they were already.

As the hours passed, the situation "normalized" and as they had a lot of free time, Susan spent it playing around and teaching bedroom secrets to Elizabeth, who enjoyed it so much that she became increasingly dependent on her company. Alice could not help but listen to the drums of moaning and laughter coming from the adjoining rooms, so she decided to ask Rapha. Making light of the matter, Rapha described them to her physically, as one would expect with quite a few defects, especially those related to the current canon of beauty, with very unfavorable details. He gossiped that the roommates had become close friends, expressing "friends" with some emphasis.

More than a dozen days had passed that seemed like weeks of such intense and vivid life. That lunch had been excessive for Rapha, he was losing sleep, so he decided to take a nap and as the heat continued, he lay down coolly in his underwear. In the middle of the dream he received an unexpected visit. The encounter with Alice had left him perplexed, disconcerted, very surprised. He thought perhaps the time had come to open up to her, tell her all, the whole truth and start from scratch. He thought about it, the pros and cons, although he could run the risk of going back on the path he had taken, and even a total break-up of relationships. He decided he could not risk it; he could not lose her. What he could do was change, improve, let the other girls live in peace, take care of them if they wanted, but focus on making Alive fall in love.

He decided to go for a ride on his motorcycle. He was euphoric and needed to burn adrenaline, he was taking a liking to circulate at high speed and alone in the desert city. He said goodbye to the rest of the girls and went down to the street, still hot, he thought that the breeze from the ride would cool him down. He knew there were certain areas of the city best not to visit so he headed for the outskirts. As he drove along, he was still excited about the subject of Alice. He was arriving at an area with narrow streets, when suddenly everything turned white, a powerful and bright light invaded everything. Without thinking, driven by his instinct, he closed his eyes, the light caused eye pain and discomfort. He lost control of the bike, zigzagged a few meters, and crashed into the stony facade of a house.

He was in a lot of pain, although he didn't lose consciousness. The landscape had gone from the purest, brightest white to the darkest, dullest black. Rapha understood immediately that the same phenomenon had occurred again, causing him to be permanently blind. The senior shouted for help, even though he knew how useless that action was, there was no one to help him. Rapha tried to stand up, although it was impossible, could not rise, he hurt all the body bruised and eroded, he noticed something wet.

"It's Gasoline," he thought.

He put his stained fingers up to his nose, but it wasn't gasoline, he smelled blood. He gently felt his abdomen and touched a soft, soggy, hot mass, it began to worry him severely, so he squeezed a bit and stood there for a few minutes. The stifling heat gradually disappeared and gradually there were terrible shivers, accompanied by an insatiable thirst. After expelling an abundant and thick vomit of semi coagulated blood, he breathed out painfully while his last thoughts evoked Alice.

Episode 2

The Security Guard

Frank heard on the walkie-talkie an Echo three complaining that it was maintenance work, not security.

"We are already with the law of minimum effort," Frank mentally lamented.

"I understand you, Echo three, but let's be practical and work together as a team. Maintenance is at the other end, we'll get there first and just flip the red switch up," he replied.

"I'm not going, it's not my job, what if the current shocks me?" Echo Three insisted.

Frank snorted, it took less time to go himself than to try to convince his useless and lazy companion.

"Don't worry, I'll go," he responded.

Always for one reason or another, it was his turn to go down to the dark depths of the basement where the entrails of the machinery that made everything work properly in the shopping center were located. He picked up the large and heavy bundle of keys which he was guarding, and down the stairs he hurried to the electric switch cabinet. He immediately located the one he was interested in and pushed it up, he wanted to check that everything was working again so Frank pressed the button on the walkie-talkie:

"Echo one for echo three, echo one for echo three."

He didn't respond.

"Echo one for echo two," he insisted again with another colleague.

The transmitter was still mute.

"Echo one for all echoes, respond."

Nothing, he re-sheathed the device. It was always the same, every time he went down to the basement there was no signal and he always ended up making a call on his private mobile. He was fed up, because it was an expense that was always on his account, the company didn't take care of those little things. He dialed Felix's private number, which was another one of his colleagues he was on duty with today, but he couldn't get through. His cell phone rang with the characteristic ringing tone, although his partner did not answer. He tried his luck with echo three, he was communicating, he tried the other colleague on duty and he couldn't get through either. It was his turn to go back upstairs, he hoped that the problem had been solved, it was very common, all the shops turned the air conditioning on full blast and at the end the electric power safety switch went off.

Frank was the group leader of the security guard company that was hired in the big shopping center of a well-known French firm. The center had a privileged location, very close to a beach on the Mediterranean Sea. Frank had a lot of experience because of his seniority, he was very professional, had a lot of self-control, and almost never lost his temper. He was very big and his graying beard instilled security, confidence and tranquility. His tone of voice was soft but firm at the same time, he always addressed his interlocutor with the utmost politeness and respect. He had a great capacity for organization and was highly respected by his colleagues and by his bosses. On many occasions he had solved serious problems, both for his colleagues and for the company. One of his bosses always commented that thanks to the knee injury that had kept him away from the national police competition in his youth, he had won over the best of his employees.

He went up the stairs somewhat irritated.

"Where could these be?" he wondered.

But as he opened the heavy fireproof door he was stunned by the sight in his eyes. The shopping center was in tremendous chaos, the unintelligible shouting was deafening, the customers were wandering slowly along the corridors colliding with the shelves and scattering all manner of goods. The different spilled liquids invaded the floor causing all kinds of comical falls, in some areas the broken glass bottles caused injuries of different severity depending on the luck in the fall of the affected.

On the escalators, there was a riot, both up and down. At the automatic entry and exit doors, the many people who had fallen to the ground were trampled by another avalanche trying to get out to the outside parking lot, ignoring the fact that the exit was half blocked by a fire caused by the collision of two vehicles. Several people were hit by the flames as they were pushed by the crowd.

The image was dantesque and Frank could not react, he remained motionless, dumbfounded and amazed. Like someone who watches a movie and is stunned by its special effects. He didn't understand anything, if just a few minutes before he had gone down to the basement and everything remained in absolute normality, what had happened there for such a lack of control?

His eye-eye was brought back to reality when the tapping of one of the customers pulled him out of the limbo where he was. His brain began to work quickly, trying to remember what he had learned in the different courses with which he was trained to practice his profession, which was complicated to apply the theory. One word hammered into his thoughts, "priorities, priorities, priorities". The man began to quickly evaluate the different dangers and tried to order them by scale of danger. He decided to tackle first the fire that partially prevented the main exit, took an extinguisher and went there, but he could not access, the door was collapsed. He went to a service door and went outside, when arrived he tried to focus the extinguisher on the vehicles although his instinct forced him to aim at the people who were still burning. The capacity of the fire extinguisher was immediately exhausted without achieving any of its purposes. The fire was growing in size and threatening to spread, he needed help and knew the protocols, he had to activate the PIDs, first intervention teams according to the procedure of the emergency plan of the mall, of which, ironically, and he was one of its members. Frank called for the station searching for colleagues without result, insisted and only Felix answered, although among so much noise pollution he only managed to understand inconsistencies about the darkness and the lack of light and something about his eyes.

"To hell with the protocols," he said, picking up his cell phone while dialing the fire department's phone number.

"Please be advised that there is currently a network overload, please call back in a few minutes."

He tried several times, all to no avail.

"Fucking country, that's how we're doing," he cursed.

Frank went to the wall, broke the protective glass and unscrewed the hose, pointed at the source of the fire, turned the tap and the strong pressure of the water flowed in a torrent through his mouth, destabilizing him and diverting the jet to one side, grabbing the hose more tightly and correcting the trajectory. He managed to suffocate it and in passing he bathed the burning people around him, he approached them and their condition was pitiful with severe burns, the clothes stuck to the skin in some cases, in others blisters or absence of skin.

He typed in the mobile again, this time the number of the health services, the ringing tone sounded but on the other end of the line nobody answered.

The moans of those people drilled into his ears, one of the ladies, with half a shaved head from the heat and a disfigured face, was looking at Frank with a strange look, as if she were absent or lost, Frank looked her straight in the eyes while she extended her hand begging for help. He was hesitant while watching that scene, remembering what he had studied in the many courses he had participated in, in the rules of the triage, very, very much to his regret, he abandoned her to the fatal fate.

The fellow felt helpless, there he did not know what else he could do, so he went to the avalanche at the entrance, to try to bring order. He approached the group of people trying to stop them and calm them down, but his voice was muffled by the hysterical noise, they could not even hear him. He made a drastic decision, turned around, and from the inside operated the controls of the automatic doors and tried to close them, only partially succeeding as several bodies lay inert on the ground blocking them. He had to turn around again and remove the bodies from the outside, thus clearing the path of the glass doors. At last the doors were joined and blocked, the main door was secured, preventing some from crushing others.

He went back inside and observed that other people continued to move around aimlessly, creating dangerous situations for themselves and others. He sighed deeply and walked down the first corridor to try to dialogue with the first client. As he approached, he noticed that something was happening to his eyes, they were closed even though his eyelids blinked with a strange movement, as if he wanted to open them but something prevented him from doing so. Also, from the tears, abundant and thick legumes were flowing and oozing. He tried to explain that it was better for him to keep his position and not wander, even to sit and be patient, until the situation improved. The individual did not listen to him, partly because of the noise and partly because of his state of nerves, he ignored Frank and continued with his wandering. He tried with the next two, he found the same ocular problems, and he got even worse result than the previous one. They grabbed him tightly, like two bathers about to drown in a raging sea, crying out for help in desperation, as if the level of help was directly proportional to the volume of his vocal cords. It cost him a button and a tear in his uniformed shirt.

"This is useless," he said as he watched the hundreds, perhaps thousands, of figures wandering through the many corridors of the department store.

This was not the way to work, if he wanted his help to be more effective, to serve a purpose, if he wanted to take control or force a turn of events, he needed to make a drastic change in the situation.

Frank took several deep breaths, cleared his throat, thought for a few moments, and holding his station firmly, pressed the code which connected with the general public address and set about making a reassuring speech:

"ATTENTION, ATTENTION, ATTENTION, PLEASE GENTLEMEN, PAY ATTENTION!"

"PLEASE BE CALM, THE EMERGENCY SERVICES ARE ON THEIR WAY, REMAIN STILL AND IMMOBILE TO AVOID POSSIBLE ACCIDENTS!"

"PLEASE REMAIN SILENT SO THAT THE STAFF WHO WILL ASSIST YOU CAN WORK COMFORTABLY, THANK YOU VERY MUCH FOR YOUR ATTENTION!"

He was sweaty and exhausted, I needed a break, time to think. At least his speech started to work, most of the clients obeyed and remained motionless, the environmental noise dropped considerably, only children's cries and a constant murmur could be heard. Thanks to this moment of relaxation, he noticed that the station was broadcasting a call from Felix who was speaking to him in an alarming tone.

"Frank, come and help me, I'm in the central box, come quickly!"

He ran over there and found Felix sitting on the floor, leaning his back on the counter. Next to him was Elisa, the hypermarket employee who was on duty that morning at the central checkout. Both of them, their eyes lost in the infinite, had the same symptoms as the others. Frank came up to him and asked about what had happened. Felix, who was very nervous, grabbed his arm and shot him with a shot that made it impossible for him to assimilate the words.

"Calm, calm, Felix, slowly, tell me everything calmly so that I can find out," Frank asked.

Getting calmer, Felix explained that everything was going well, except for the suffocating heat caused by the breakdown of the air conditioning. In an instant, a very powerful light invaded everything, like a gigantic flash from a big camera. Instinctively he closed his eyes, seconds later he could no longer keep them open and everything remained in absolute darkness. He did not know what had happened and why he was blind, and he sensed that the same thing was happening to everyone else. Elisa described it in a similar way, adding that they had a lot of discomfort inside their eyes, as if a sand blast from the beach had hit them directly in the face.

"Felix, we're going to try to get help, you're going to do the following, pick up your cell phone and call the police, the fire department, and the ambulance service. If you don't succeed, you try again and again, insisting and insisting, we need more people to help here."

"But Frank," he replied, "how do I dial if I don't see the numbers?"

"It's true, I'm sorry, I hadn't realized."

He thought for a few seconds and found the solution.

"Take my mobile, I have the numbers memorized by voice dialing, just say out loud 'police', 'fire' or 'ambulance', wait, I'll prepare it for you, try it."

Felix began his task, not managing to contact anyone in the first moments.

"Well, you, Elisa, here's the megaphone, here's the talk button. If you hear people getting nervous or the rumor gets too loud, you give them a reassuring message. Above all, I need you to stay put and be as quiet as possible."

"I'm going to go for a walk and see what else I can do, I'll be back in a bit."

He hurried off to the drink aisle, evacuating amidst intense protests by pushing or dragging the passers-by he found there. He blocked the two entrances, one with a cleaning trolley and the other with a large basket containing textiles, he didn't want any more injuries from glass cuts.

Frank felt fortunate to be in the basement at the precise moment of the wave of light, but he also felt sorry for the weight of responsibility that was coming upon him. How could he alone help and care for thousands of people, it was impossible, how would he feed them, how would he find them accommodation or comfort, and the sick and wounded, besides, what if the whole city was affected, or the whole country, or the whole world? It could be the end of civilization as we know it today.

A huge weight of grief came over him, he panicked, for a few minutes he was assailed by the idea of running away and leaving everything, so everything would be easier. To maintain his survival would not be very difficult and even that of a small group of friends and colleagues affected, besides, he was just a simple security guard. Although something inside him prevented him from continuing with that idea, he calmed down and thought that perhaps the phenomenon was only happening here and in a few hours help would come from other places. He decided to go in parts without anticipating events, first solve the problems in the mall and get immediate help.

By chance he was at the doors of the mall's cinema, where several films were being shown in the morning. As a rule, the theatres were not open in the morning, but that week there was a special promotion, morning premiere films at reduced prices. He got excited, he looked for the cinema employee at the box office, there sitting in his armchair John was waiting for someone to take him out since he was locked up. For security reasons the box office was locked from the inside, but he couldn't find the keys. Frank spotted them in a corner of the shelf and guided John towards them and not without difficulty he managed to open the door.

"John, are there people watching movies, take me to the projection room," he ordered.

Frank stopped the screenings and it didn't take long for the movie theater patrons to kick, whistle and protest energetically. Everyone was fine, none of them were affected. He went from room to room and with a lot of patience he had to explain several times the situation they were in. He implored them and begged for urgent help, some accepted without hesitation, others got into a sterile debate and the rest left with various excuses. They returned to the central corridor and Frank began to coordinate his small army, he had managed to gather about two hundred and fifty people. He asked if there was a doctor or a nurse, there was luck, five people raised their hands. He pointed to a corner where the mattress stand was located, so that they could attend to the wounded there. The necessary material could be provided in the corridor of the drugstore and in the pharmacy, and the others who found the wounded or sick, except for the blindness, could bring them there.

He made teams of three and instructed that all affected personnel be taken out into the center aisle and seated at the edges. Another group was asked to take care of the needs of those who were arriving, taking them to the toilets, as some were already defecating and urinating in the corridors. Giving them water or some food was another task, another group was asked to do a sweep of the office area and bring the employees, and another group was asked the same but in the catering area on the second floor.

"Hey, I need you to take those cleaning carts and collect all the glass, dry the liquids spilled on the floor, and please, including urine and 'similar', thank you very much."

He asked Felix if he had managed to contact anyone, and he answered in denial, so he sent another group to a nearby police station for official help. For this mission he opened the doors of the shopping center and took the opportunity to ask other teams to help the people in the car park.

"Elisa use the megaphone, reassure the people again and tell them that help is already here and that they should collaborate as much as possible. If someone needs something, to eat or drink, to go to the toilet or something else, they will have to raise their hand like when we were at school, they will be attended to as soon as possible."

That was already something else, Frank was in his element, and he was beginning to have the situation under control. He gave a tour of inspection and was ordering details from one and all. But when he arrived at the infirmary the harsh reality slapped his senses, he did not expect so many wounded and the colophon was given to him by one of the nurses when he asked him the procedure to follow with respect to the dead. Again he felt overwhelmed, he did not know how to solve this problem, he just thought of parking it, for the moment he ordered other groups to put them in the back yard, in the access esplanade of the trucks, he would think later on how to solve it. The nurse also told him that they had brought him a girl in a great state of anxiety who had been raped. Frank was left speechless, not knowing what to say, they didn't have enough problems, and on top of that, before even trying to address that problem his attention was urgently requested:

"Frank, Frank!"

One of his anonymous assistants was hurrying to warn him, he didn't know his name, it was impossible for him to memorize them all in such a short time.

"You have to see this, the group from the police station is coming."

It was good news, he could finally unload this heavy burden, step aside and hand over the responsibilities to the experts. He looked out the door and what he saw impressed him, almost the whole police station was coming...

A long line of dark blue uniforms, linked to each other by hand, advanced slowly, in fits and starts, led by the group sent by Frank. When they arrived they were accommodated in the little space available, the mall was beginning to become saturated.

He congratulated them on the great idea of making human chains to move groups, and genius the use of the "phone game" as a method to communicate the unevenness or anomalies of the road. The group of newcomers explained to Frank that the situation outside was much worse than theirs, everything they had found was blind, injured or dead. They told him that the streets were impassable, clogged by vehicles stopped in any way, plus multiple collisions and even some fires and explosions. He wanted to contact someone in charge of the police station, but most of them remained shocked, morally depressed by the new and depressing situation in which they found themselves. Frank had to forget about the police, firemen, ambulances, Civil Protection or the army.

The responsibility and problems extended to the whole city and they planned again to land on Frank's shoulders and back. He had doubts again, what was he doing there, he was nobody to assume the functions of a leader. He felt like going home, relaxing and forgetting about the problems. It was easier to step aside and let others who were more prepared take his place, but who, if there were hardly any people left who were not blind, what if this new leader did not make the right decisions? He could not take that risk, he could not leave those poor blind people to their fate, he would at least ensure that everything possible would be done to keep them safe.

Again focused on his task, he gathered his collaborators and showed them the raw and hard reality. He encouraged them to continue with their important work, sowing the altruistic seed of responsibility, civility and commitment to others. In short, they were to expand and continue their humanitarian work, little by little, throughout the city.

Most of the young people expressed their disagreement, claiming that they had family, friends and colleagues who also needed help. They were worried about them and wanted to come to their aid. This was a problem for Frank's plans, it meant that when he left, the few human resources he had would be diluted and with few people he could do little to help the population. He energetically showed his anger, labeled them as uncivil, selfish and unsupportive, the discussion was getting more and more heated, some began to march and he could not keep them, so he devised an intermediate plan in an instant. He gently lowered the tone of the controversy and agreed to their demands, expressing his agreement and inviting them to go and rescue their relatives. But he begged them to go back with them to the mall, where they already had a small infrastructure set up, with food and a small clinic. They would have their relatives attended and controlled, and they could also continue helping the rest of the city. The great majority thought it was a magnificent idea and they all marched in a hurry in different directions, promising to return and recruit new helpers if they found more sighted ones.

Frank then decided to reorganize the big hypermarket a little better with the few that were left, he asked for a couple of volunteers with administrative skills and told them to go to the computer section, choose a laptop and take two censuses, one of sighted and one of blind people. He asked them to collect the data of all the staff, their names, dates of birth and work or knowledge of those who could be useful, so that at some point they could be used as consultants. In addition to having control of how many people we trained, we avoided leaving anyone forgotten and they had to write down every new person who joined.

Another group was sent to the opticians and ordered to requisition all the sunglasses and hand them out, first to the sighted and then to everyone else. He wanted everyone with sunglasses permanently, it could not be ruled out that the phenomenon would be repeated, although he did not know how effective it was, he felt that this precaution was better than nothing. Besides, it was disgusting every time he contemplated the sick eyes of the blind ones, at least he would avoid the unpleasant view, although he did not share with anyone this observation.

He asked others to roam around the neighborhood and, using the effective method of the human chain, to save as many of the neighbors as possible. The man looked for several maps of the city and studied them carefully, choosing large buildings with large spaces: Sports Pavilion, Football Stadium, Libraries, Hospital, City Hall, Museums, Institutes and Schools. He would use these buildings as evacuation centers, divide the city into zones and assign an action zone for each public building. He would meditate on how to arrange brigades for the different tasks to be carried out. He would need to clear the main streets of the city of vehicles to have greater mobility, and appropriate vehicles to move affected people, food and belongings. Another group of collaborators should mitigate fires, minimize risks and secure the city, such as possible gas leaks, check gas stations, they just had to fight another series of cataclysms.

In the long run, the deaths would also be a problem, after a few days the rot would be present and the risk of disease evident. But he thought that burying them would consume a lot of resources, so he decided that the most agile thing would be to burn them in a big bonfire and the most suitable place would be the cemetery esplanade.

"At least we should try to identify all the bodies so that we can inform their families," he comforted himself aloud.

It was getting dark and the number of those rescued was increasing, quite a few collaborators were keeping their promise and were returning.

Frank went to the DIY section and collected flashlights, portable megaphones and battery-powered drills, a long night was coming. He gathered the sighted together to tell them their plans, fortunately they had increased in number. A smile escaped his lips, some boys looked ridiculous with female sunglasses, and apparently they had not had any luck with the delivery. He formed several groups, distributed the material and assigned tasks, areas and public buildings. Also, he showed them how to pick a lock with a drill and ordered them to get going. Moreover, the fellow assigned himself the area closest to the shopping center, his evacuation point was the Sports Pavilion, and this area was very central, with high buildings and large population. They would first carry out a raid in the streets to clear the streets of those affected, as these were the weakest and most defenseless ones. As soon as they were able to go through the buildings one by one, he deduced that the people who remained in their homes had a much better chance of surviving since they knew their environment much better, their own homes gave them security and they could feed themselves for a few days with the food accumulated in their pantries, these people according to his list of priorities would take second place.

The streets were crowded with blind citizens. After calming them down, they were advised to link their hand with the one next to them and then walk slowly following the instructions of the companion who was ahead of them to overcome obstacles, so that little by little they formed long columns that went towards the Sports Pavilion. When they reached the entrance of the pavilion they drilled the lock to open the doors. Fortunately, the cataclysm had not affected the electricity and water services, and after lighting the rooms, they prepared all the personnel as best they could. They broke into a nearby grocery store and handed out a frugal snack. It was dawn and they were so tired that they fell asleep right away.

Frank woke up in the late afternoon, that agonizing look of that lady consumed by fire, with the skin of her face in tatters, had appeared to her in the form of a nightmare.

In the ward the bustle had started hours ago. Everything was calm and under control, one of the assistants approached him and told about one of the rescued people who was in the shopping center, who was blind.

"What a surprise, like everyone else," Frank said.

"No, I mean he was blind before, he's been blind since birth."

"So?"

"Well Frank, I know James by sight, he used to sell coupons on the streets years ago. But he has special training, his advice, experience and help can be very useful. Above all on how we should handle the rest of the blind people and he can teach them how to face their new situation."

"You are right, it seems to me very good, that they should set up a work area for him here and he should get on with it, thank you."

"Oh, another thing, we have been given a list of ointments from the hospital area which an ophthalmologist advises for the eye treatment of those affected.

"Well, I'll have a team check the pharmacies in the area to find them."

"Frank!" another assistant called.

"Goddamn it, stop harassing me! I haven't even had breakfast!" Frank shouted angrily.

"But..." he answered in a daze.

"You can't do anything by yourselves? This isn't mine, I don't own the town, I'm nobody."

"I'm sorry," he apologized, "I just wanted to talk to you about something."

"No, you forgive me, it's just that I haven't had a good rest," Frank apologized ashamedly, "tell me."

"It turns out we couldn't find sunglasses for everyone."

"The sighted have preference, they are the basis for taking care of others," he answered somewhat being more relaxed."

"Yes, OK, but as we are not sure how effective the measure is, and in view of the possibility that the event will be repeated, to avoid greater evils, it had occurred to me that in order not to take risks, it would be best not to stay in the daytime as much as possible and to act as much as possible at night. Perhaps that would mean changing our habits a little, at least for a while."

Frank thought for a few seconds and then added:

"I think it's a wonderful idea. Until we have more information about this abnormality, we will proceed like this. It would even be interesting to protect the interiors of the buildings we use from the light, we would have to place dense curtains on the windows or something similar."

From now on they would work preferably at night, the days would follow one another quickly, and so much short for the enormous and arduous work that consumed them. The hours were devoured by the many tasks and problems that beset them.

With the excuse of examining pharmacies he decided to take a walk outside, take a look around and try to calm down and relax. He waited for the sunset to leave, chose a companion and went out in search of pharmaceutical material especially that related to ophthalmology. When they entered one of the pharmacies they came across a stubby little man, bald and with high prescription glasses.

"Are you all right, I mean can you see?" asked Frank, the question contained a certain irony, considering the thickness of his glasses.

"Yes, of course I see well, I'm not blind, are you?" the man replied.

Frank answered, although it was obvious that they were not blind, they introduced themselves, and the little man was called Rapha. Frank explained his achievements, that they were a group of unaffected people and that they were willing to help most of the blind ones. He proposed that he join them as they needed all the help they could get, they could not wait for the government's help as the problem affected the whole country. In that area they had the evacuation point in the Sports Pavilion, many people had to be fed and the streets cleaned of corpses, to avoid epidemics and disease. Rapha agreed, but he had a small group of people he kept safe, would pick them up and head to the pavilion soon.

Rapha told them that he had seen people, he could not say how many, robbing and destroying shops, raping a girl, and ignoring blind people by denying them any assistance. Frank was disturbed by the news of the existence of gangs, scavengers willing to take advantage of the weakness of others. He had not contemplated that contingency, so from now on they had to take extreme precautions.

"See you in a bit, see you later," said Rapha.

Frank and his companion continued with their task, they looked for the ointments of ophthalmology from the list that the doctor had given them, but they found the empty spaces, there was nothing, something strange they had no choice but to go to another pharmacy. As they walked through the shadows, Frank began to be more cautious, remaining alert to any strange movements. The news of the gangs left him worried, he was even thinking, very seriously, about the possibility of getting weapons.

When he returned, he looked for the little man who had given them the information, in order to gather data with more accuracy. He needed to know if he remembered if that gang carried weapons and what kind, in which part of town he saw them, if he found them once or several times, approximate number of members. His search was unsuccessful, he didn't find him there. He contacted the other evacuation points, alerting them to the danger of finding undesirables and giving them a description of the little man who had alerted them because he needed to interrogate them.

A few days later, they heard nothing more about the man, and since they could not corroborate his information, he dismissed the idea of firearms. In inexperienced hands they would be more harmful than beneficial, he did handle small arms, since for work reasons he had a license that obliged him at least once a year to go for shooting practice. He would try to get one for safety, but for the others, at most a bat or baseball bat, he decided to wait for more news of other contacts with these gangs.

After several days of accumulated tiredness, continuous problems and exhaustion were making a dent on Frank, his character was increasingly surly and irascible.

"Frank, I've been told that last night another couple of blocks in the downtown area were left in the dark," one of the psychics reported.

"And what do you want me to do? I'm not a fucking electrician and we don't have any operatives!" he replied in an increasingly assiduous tone.

"He said it so you would know, as you always have good ideas."

"Well, now I can't think of any!"

"Right, now I can't think of any, there's a quarter of the city without electricity, if we go on like this we'll soon be completely in the dark, everything will stop working, and our situation will get worse, but worse," he responded.

"The most sensible thing is to spread the word, find the Electric Company workers and get them to tell us how to solve the problem," said another member of the group."

"Very well thought out," the others chanted.

Frank got angry with himself for not falling for such a simple solution.

Another of his assistants remained there, mute and distressed.

"What about you? Don't you have homework to do?"

"I just…"

"What? Let go now, I cannot spend the whole afternoon with this."

"The supplies from the big supermarkets are running out, there's hardly any fresh fruit and vegetables left, what little there is has started to rot."

"God!" he exclaimed as he sat down.

"We could look for more stores. And we could do the same, ask the blind if they know of any stores we don't know about,' he pointed out again."

"Hey, I'll give you my seat, truly," Frank pleaded.

"Frank, this isn't about positions, it isn't about you carrying all the weight, it's about all of us being a team and doing our part to solve our many problems," he said as he put one hand on the other man's shoulder in friendship.

"You are right, you are right, but today I am particularly discouraged," Frank was honest, "we had improved somewhat, but it was a short term improvement, like a mirage, in the long term I do not see good expectations. We need help. What will happen when there are no more warehouses to loot?"

"We can go to the greenhouses and to the farms to harvest the crops already sown," said another.

"For that we would need a lot of manpower, because we need many kilos of vegetables and fruit for all the thousands of people who have been taken in," said Frank.

"We can take the blind with us and let them do it."

"We need buses, lorries, drivers, staff to guide them and explain to them, we are already very few, we can hardly look after them here. I see it as very complicated," added Frank.

"The phones are already working, at first they stopped working because of the saturation of calls, and the lines were blocked. One of us should try to call other cities, Madrid, to know what the real situation is in the rest of the country," commented another of the group, "maybe there is help somewhere in the country."

"Yes, that's not a bad idea, we'll have to try, we're going to get going," he said.

When he was alone, he thought more deeply about all these problems, decided that he would start rationing food and that blind people should start getting more involved in helping. He took up the idea of taking them to the crops, they didn't have to go and take them every day. It was more sensible to take a large group there and provide them with housing in one of the many agricultural buildings surrounding the fields. Frank did not know this, but perhaps he was planting the idea of a society based on a semi-slavery of the blind.

To relax, he decided to go on another raid that night. After so many days, there was little hope of finding someone to help, although he would not stay, he would try again.

They decided to go for a walk around the center as they had not been there for many days. They were driving slowly, observing some anomaly, some movement, silent to hear better something out of the ordinary. Suddenly someone ordered them to stop, they had heard a sound. They stopped the engine and paid special attention for a few seconds, in the distance there was almost imperceptible music. They got out and walked around looking for the murmur to come closer, they walked several blocks and the song was getting louder.

They continued to approach and more and more clearly, a melody of the famous David Bowie was invading the street.

Episode 3

The Blind One

I got up early, like I do every day. I live alone, I need more time to eat breakfast and get ready than the others, because the times of the seers and the blind are different. A blind person needs a little more time for normal activities. My name is James and I have been blind since birth. I have never seen the sea, nor a sunrise, nor a child, nor a smile. I have never seen the world, although life has taught me that lamenting is not worth it, nor in becoming depressed, that this is about facing and fighting it, but you need weapons if you long to combat. Moreover, I use tenacity, insistence, perseverance, work, constancy and above all memory, for which I use various techniques to improve and increase it. But the weapon that I like most of all is humor, I consider myself a horny, optimistic guy who takes life with a lot of grace. I'm one of those who knows more blind jokes, I use them as a shield, to defend myself from the non-blind, now, what I can't stand is a sighted person making fun of the blind or being made fun of in my face because of my disability, that's why I'm in a very bad mood this morning.

I work in the delegation for the disabled in Almería, a Mediterranean city in the south of the Iberian Peninsula, located in the right-hand corner of the map. I started as a coupon seller, for years I did this rewarding job, it is very entertaining. You meet a lot of people and you even get to have a certain friendship with the regulars, and if you give out prizes on top of that, that's it, I've given out a few. But I felt like a change of scenery, so with perseverance and studies I got a position in the training department.

I'm single and without a girlfriend, although every now and then I'm lucky and I hook up. And if I have a drought season, I solve it with a friend, one of those paid, high level, but always the same. I am faithful to her, we the blind people are very routine and I like her quite a lot, she always prepares dinner for me in her fresh and aromatic terrace of her attic, in fact whenever I call her to meet, we use the same contractual phrase:

"Do you 'invite' me to dinner, Susan?" and she very solicitously gives me an appointment, day and time.

It is difficult to find a woman who wants to spend her life with someone like me, if a normal marriage is already difficult, it is even more difficult with a blind man. It causes more dependence and work overload, with the handicap that I am sterile because of a voluntary vasectomy operation, restricting my possible partner's maternal instinct.

My blindness is genetic and hereditary, so it did not seem right or morally right to have children in these conditions knowing the difficulties I would have to live through. I prefer this option to the one my parents chose, abandoning me to my own fate, giving me up for adoption. As no married couple chose me, I was finally adopted by the state and a guest in special centers for many years. Although I was lucky enough to be raised in one of the best in the country, I learned almost everything I know there. But above all I learned to be as self-sufficient and autonomous as possible, I wouldn't do too badly since over the years I evolved from a student to a teacher, helping others to overcome the problems I had.

As I was saying, that morning started badly, the alarm clock didn't ring at the set time. I woke up anyway because I have the habit of getting up at the same time, although when I switched on the radio to listen to my usual news broadcast the device remained mute. Two failures at once was too much chance, I deduced that there was no electricity at home, this could be for two reasons, a general failure or a failure in the electrical installation of my apartment. I looked for the electrical panel and confirmed that the main switch was down, then I turned it up but it didn't stay there, it jumped back to the off position. I tried several times but it was still the same, there was some electrical device that blew my main switch. I started using a sieve to try to find out which device it was, so I disconnected one, went back to the electrical panel to connect the main switch and if it jumped down again it was because the unplugged device was not responsible for the failure. I performed the operation many times, I could not find the cause, and I just had to test the refrigerator and air conditioning. So I deduced that the fault was in one of the two, but I had a problem, the plug of the refrigerator was behind the appliance that was embedded in the kitchen and I could not access the plug and the air conditioner was installed on a wall almost on the ceiling. I thought it was risky to try it on my own, plus I never bought a portable ladder, so I asked for help from the doorman of the building who was always willing to help, of course in exchange for a good tip. I called him on his mobile, it was impossible because I couldn't get a line, a pre-recorded voice from the phone company kept repeating:

"We inform you that the lines are busy, try again after a few minutes."

It was getting late, I had already lost an hour and the truth is that I didn't feel like going down in my pajamas to look for the doorman. So I took a quick cold shower, first because the electric water heater wasn't working and second because I felt like it because of the heat that morning. I couldn't shave either because I am used to doing it with an electric razor or even having my classic coffee with milk and toast for breakfast either.

I left the house already a bit upset, my daily routine had been blown up. I arrived very late to the office, badly arranged, without breakfast, without my morning news, with an electrical breakdown at home that was not fixed. The doorman had not yet arrived at the building and I could not wait for him any longer, and on top of that the mobile phones were still out of order.

As I unfurled my cane, I started to walk, I was engrossed in my domestic problems, and I did not notice the demonstration until after a while. It must have been one of the big ones since there was a lot of unintelligible shouting and car horns, the thing is that I didn't remember in yesterday's news that today there would be some call for a strike or protest or rally. The truth is, what scared me was the strong smell of burning, the matter seemed important to me because I imagined that they would have built barricades of burning tires.

My instinct advised me to go home, but what was I going to do there all morning without electricity. I decided to change my route to avoid the main avenues and take a walk. This also bothered me, as I prefer the main roads because the sidewalks are wider and better suited for reduced mobility, you know, no steps at the curbs of pedestrian crossings and adapted traffic lights. Besides, they forced me to skip my daily routine again, not to mention that the street is more complicated, although in the end I took it as a new adventurous challenge. I started my journey by turning left, the sidewalk was narrower, so I deduced that the street was also narrower, no vehicles were circulating. I was walking while tracking the sidewalk with my cane, until I stumbled upon a bag of garbage that some unconscious person had dropped on the ground, unfortunately such citizens abounded in this uncivilized country. Because I held on to the greasy garbage container, I did not stamp my face on the ground, and then I heard someone screaming on the opposite sidewalk:

"I'm blind, I can't see, I can't see!"

It seemed to me a cruel mockery, so I responded with another scream:

"What's the matter, are we kidding? I don't think it's funny!"

I continued walking somewhat angrily and a few steps further on, someone sitting on the ground suddenly grabbed my ankle, which almost made me fall on my face. Miraculously, I managed to keep my balance, a young voice insisted and insisted:

"I can't see, I can't see, I'm blind!"

I hit it with all my strength on the forearm which was still holding tightly on my ankle, and after a painful scream, it let go of me. I sped up as much as I could, the joke was already getting very heavy. I didn't think it was safe today to take these less busy side streets, so I decided to go out to another main street and just as I was getting into it, someone suddenly came out of a doorway and shouted in my ear:

"Help me!"

I responded angrily:

"What, are you blind too? Another one with the little joke? Then go fuck yourself!"

And sweeping the sidewalk from side to side with my long white cane, I walked away grumbling.

The smell of smoke became more intense, I was hit by bursts of barbecue-flavored air. The great murmur became more audible and intelligible as I approached.

Another individual grabbed my arm tightly and shouted at me:

"I've gone blind, I've gone blind!"

"Well, welcome to the club, I have been blind since birth," I replied grumblingly.

"Oh, I'm sorry," he said, very surprised at the unexpected response.

"Perhaps you can help me," he continued, "the other people I met were blind like me."

"Could you take me to the medical center?" he asked in a hesitant tone.

"Of course I could take you, I know the center of the city quite well, there is a clinic behind the shopping center," I answered almost offended.

"But what has happened to you?" I continued to question him with curiosity.

The man told me about the events that had happened to him that morning. How he was suddenly made blind by an unknown and powerful ambient light that invaded everything. From what he told me he was not the only one affected, with all the people he had encountered they were all in the same situation. I believed him and understood that what had happened to me during my journey was not a matter of jokers, but certainly more affected. At that moment I felt a bit embarrassed about my previous behavior. I instructed the stranger to walk behind me, put his hand on my shoulder, and listen to my verbal commands to avoid obstacles and go up or down steps.

Every now and then we met someone who was affected, who joined our entourage, and who was gradually getting longer. At one point I lost track of how many of us were in that strange group of blind fools. Thus, all of us in a chain went to the shopping center area. The formerly peaceful walk became a long and painful journey. It was difficult to move forward, every few minutes I had to overcome new obstacles, or a vehicle had invaded the sidewalk, or someone unconscious or in worse condition was blocking it.

Moving through a clearer street a curious thought came to my mind, I stopped and questioned my followers.

"Give me more details, your mental image, when you try to see, is it total black or milky-like white?" I raised my voice.

"It's totally black," said one.

"Black," replied another.

"I can't see anything at all," said someone in the background.

"Milky-like white? I don't understand the question," said just another blinded man.

The murmur of misunderstanding became unintelligible.

"Keep calm, please, it's all right. I was just trying to rule out an absurd theory based on Saramago's books."

"Who's that, a famous doctor?" asked an unknown voice.

"You have to read more, less TV and more books," I replied with irony.

Again an incomprehensible debate that I stopped by starting the march.

"Forget it, I didn't say anything, it doesn't matter," I said to my direct follower who obediently passed on my message to the one behind me.

We approached an important avenue and again the screams, sounds and smells dazed my senses and every time I stumbled upon someone, we stopped. They told us the repetitive story, that they had gone blind, their repetitive desperate request for help, again my repetitive explanations, my repetitive proposal and my repetitive instructions. The progress through the city was becoming more and more painful and slower, it was going to take us forever to reach the medical center. A few long hours had passed and I was still fasting. My stomach was reminding me that I was late in getting hungry, so preventing the health center from having food to put in my mouth, I decided to stop inside the shopping center to relieve my appetite. Then we would continue to the already very close health center. We finally managed to get to the Shopping Centre, although we had to make a small and unexpected detour, as we found that the main door was closed. We had no choice but to look for one of the side doors to access our new destination.

A great murmur and rumor set the hypermarket in motion. As we entered slowly, the loudspeaker, in a very manly voice and at a very high volume, thundered a message in a reassuring tone:

"ATTENTION, ATTENTION, ATTENTION, PLEASE GENTLEMEN, PAY ATTENTION!"

"PLEASE BE CALM, THE EMERGENCY SERVICES ARE ON THEIR WAY, REMAIN STILL AND INMOBILE TO AVOID POSSIBLE ACCIDENTS!"

"PLEASE REMAIN SILENT SO THAT THE STAFF WHO WILL ASSIST YOU CAN WORK COMFORTABLY, THANK YOU VERY MUCH FOR YOUR ATTENTION!"

Change of plans, we no longer needed to go near the medical center, those gentlemen would from now on take care of the well-being of my many companions. I felt more relieved and comforted, finally good news, I followed the instructions and moved to the side of the corridor next to a shelf. My entourage imitated me, I advised the one following me that it was best to sit down and wait, to pass on the message. I sat down on the floor at the foot of the shelf, I was hungry, so I tried my luck and I stretched out my arm towards the product that was sold at this point, by the touch of the bag and its crunching sound I knew it was chips, I decided to open it and kill the bug.

It had been many hours and I was bored enough. Inactivity kills me, so I decided to offer my services, I had dedicated many years to this task, it was the best asset at that time, and the best way to help in this difficult situation. But that guy didn't find my proposal interesting, besides he knew me from my time as a coupon seller, from when I walked the streets with my beautiful guide dog, Once (so it was called as the acronym of the Spanish organization for blind people) was its name, that poor guy died of old age, I haven't cried in my life anymore, so much so that I decided that he would be the first and the last one, never again. The sales tour on the streets was not the same anymore, besides everybody was asking me about Once, I was constantly reminded of his absence, that was the trigger to change my life, to run away from the streets and return to studies.

My interlocutor replied with disinterest that they had enough problems to solve and tasks to perform, as to be wasting time on nonsense. I had to prove to him the validity of my proposal so I only gave him a simple example. I challenged him to simulate explaining to a blind man how to face a step. He accepted with a sly laugh, as he thought it was a fairly simple test.

"Get closer, slowly, very slowly," he began his explanation with little interest, "Be careful, there is a step, don't fall down, stand up, put your foot up, put it down carefully, now put your other foot up and put it next to the other one, that's it."

All those present laughed in a mocking tone, I waited patiently for them to finish, and when the room was silent, I began with my reply.

"I caught you, smarty-pants," I thought with an inner smile.

"All right, that's fine and might do it, which would be one of the many options to help a blind man get over the obstacle of a step. Perhaps someone else would have chosen to pick him up, jump over the step, and then lay him down on the floor" all laughed at my thought.

"But there are details in your explanation which are vital and important for the safety of a blind person, and you have omitted them," I explained, leaving a halo of mystery floating in the air.

Everyone was expectant and thoughtful, looking for the solution to my enigma. After a few seconds of waiting, I unraveled the mystery with a question:

"Is the step you have described ascending or descending? if the step was descending you have caused our poor blind friend to fall down the stairs... You know they are not approached in the same way, they are quite different!"

There was a murmur of recognition from those present, so I took the opportunity to finish off the job with a line of "how good and clever I am".

"And details like this can be found in many situations, and I have to warn you, with modesty, that I am a specialist, so you will see."

"And in addition to organizing courses for blind people for sighted ones, I am also able to give courses for blind people for new blind ones."

"I'm also an expert in Tiflotechnology. And since no one has any idea what that is, I will explain to you that it is the branch of science that studies applied technology as an aid to the visually impaired, from technical aids for everyday life to high technology and adapted computer programs."

After a deathly silence, that individual admitted defeat and agreed to my proposal.

"I need several sighted people to help me, as well as a well-equipped classroom with a series of tools such as long canes, auxiliary instruments for measuring and controlling time, light alarms, talking colour detectors, talking compasses, talking label readers, electronic reading instruments and access to information such as text-to-speech converters, Reading edge and Optacon, a Perkins machine, a Braille line, digital diaries..."

"Stop, stop," he interrupted me suddenly, "I don't know what it is and where to find all the material you are listing. Perhaps I haven't grasped the level of chaos we are in, we have no means and no staff. We have many priorities, such as covering basic needs like food, health and security."

"Your help," he continued in his sermon, "will be very welcome, but in principle you will have to adapt to organizing a series of short and simple seminars of a couple of hours each. First of all to teach all the sighted people, in turn, how to improve the way they relate to the blind ones, as well as to learn how to protect them better. Then you will start your work with the blind and I can only assign you one sighted person to help you."

I sighed deeply, accepting with resignation, but I asked him to please assign me a girl. I get along better with the female gender, I find them more affable, careful and detail-oriented when working with them.

"I also need an Anti-Triffids suit," I said jokingly.

"An anti-what suit?" he asked, having no idea what I was talking about.

"No, nothing, forget about it, it's smart humor."

"I don't understand you, are you calling me a fool?"

"No, no, sorry, but if you don't know Wyndham and his work you won't get the joke."

"Well, explain it to me."

"It doesn't matter, it's a long story, and it's blind man's stuff, stuff we say to each other in my group of friends."

He left while being a little annoyed, but he ordered me to be transferred to the Sports Hall. In the rooms assigned to me I began to teach my notions, improvising, in the short time I had, some simple and summarized lessons.

Beginning with the rules of behavior, the way to introduce yourself and identify yourself, such as greeting and tone of voice. Generally, blind people hear very well, and even better, as the rest of their senses are improved, made more sensitive and enhanced, so it is not necessary to raise your voice to talk to them. We will introduce ourselves with our name and the reason why we contacted them.

It is useless to use gestures, on the contrary we must use them very carefully and be quite specific with the verbal language. Above all offer details when pointing out the situation of objects, nothing from here or there, we must provide information about the spatial situation of the object and even lead his hand. We can use verbs and visual terms without problems, they will not be hurt in their feelings, on the contrary we must try to normalize as much as possible.

If in the talk we are going to sit down we will approach them to a chair and placing your hand on the back we will indicate that they have it right in front.

We must tell them if we go out or enter the room, it is important to order them and maintain the following safety rules. All the objects must keep their usual position and if they are changed we must indicate it, the doors and windows totally closed or totally open, the chairs under the table or stuck to the wall, not dispersed, the doors and drawers of the closets closed too.

They must be trained in household tasks and personal hygiene, as they are in danger of hurting themselves or others.

It is also very important to help them to move, the sighted person will offer the elbow to the blind person who places the hand on top, in the inner arm area. The guide will go half a step ahead so that the blind person will notice the changes in speed, avoiding sudden movements and when climbing stairs we will indicate if it is up or down, we will always go one step ahead of him and when the guide finishes he will wait for the blind person to finish going down or up.

We will help them to strengthen their touch, hearing and kinesthesia perception, as well as the handling of the cane. With touch they will learn to locate, discriminate and recognize shapes, detect sizes, weights, textures and temperatures. With the ear they can learn to detect and avoid obstacles, appreciate distances and warn of dangers. With kinesthesia they learn with movement if there are slopes or curves, to maintain balance and straight line, to control turns, to know if they reach the target, if there are irregularities in the terrain.

With the cane they learn to move with more autonomy, detecting with enough time and thus be able to avoid all the obstacles, works, ditches that are in the lower part.

I have to admit that in spite of the circumstances, that stage of my life was splendid, because thanks to my effort and my quality as a teacher, I was able to improve the quality of life of many people. And curiously, to go through life somewhat anonymously, although many people heard my voice from my time as a salesman, from now on I would become a very influential, popular and beloved character of my city, we go what is said a celebrity.

And to top it all off, among those classes, little by little, almost without noticing it, like a crystalline stream that winds through a slight slope to, at the end, flow into a placid lake. This is how my love story with my assistant Rachel developed. We got on very well, we understood each other fantastically well, and we immediately empathized. Then a few laughs, lively conversations, the touch of our hands, a few stumbles, a few confidences, a few whispers. We had a lot of complicity, without forgetting my great verbosity, which generated magnificent speeches. I managed to take her to my bed, what a scandal! We did not enjoy any intimacy, and her moans woke up half a pavilion. Luckily, we pretended to be there, and only those closest to us knew where the commotion was coming from. She told me that she had never enjoyed herself so much, she missed me a lot, I just did what I always do, maybe she was from few encounters, few experiences. The fact is that her admiration and fascination for me increased. So the relationship was already filmed, but for our next and intimate encounters, we were more discreet and looked for more solitary places.

And ironies of life, I, who got a vasectomy myself for fear of my paternity, to avoid raising blind children. In the end, together with my sweet Rachel, we ended up adopting a wonderful child, one of the many little blind orphans caused by that terrible catastrophe.

Episode 4

The Doctor

At the moment, I do not like the night shifts, at the beginning I endured them, although there is always work, there is a little less than during the day. There's more free time, you have fun chatting with colleagues, reading, working on the computer or looking at things on the Internet. But as the years go by, the sleepless nights take their toll, now it's harder for me to stay awake. The few free moments I have are spent nodding off and taking short naps on the uncomfortable examination table in my hospital emergency room.

When you start studying medicine, you make the decision because you like it, you have plenty of job opportunities, you will earn a good salary, you will help many people, and you will save and heal lives.

You don't stop to think that sickness and accidents don't have timetables, that they can happen on Sundays and holidays, day and night, you discover this handicap after a few years of work.

When a new patient arrives, they knock on my door or give me a "pager" call. It has just gone off, so I get up, get up in the sink with some fresh water, do a bit of rewashing and in a minute I'm in the critical care room, finding out the cause of the emergency. The assiduous nurses already have the patient prepared in a nightgown and with an intravenous line, it is an autolysis. I hate these cases, I understand that human beings are attacked by viruses, bacteria, infections, or that they are victims of accidents, whether they are fortuitous, traffic or similar. But I will never understand these cases of attempted suicide, I consider them as extra work, work that should not be done. If a suicidal person made a good attempt, he would be a corpse and would not cause an overload of work in the emergency room.

The patient is in his forties, quite bald, overweight and short in height. Not a very visually pleasing guy, really. He's unconscious, I need information on what medications and how many he's taken. I'm informed that in the bathroom of his house the ambulance crew found an empty bottle of a known antidepressant. I order an injection to bring him back to consciousness, after causing him great pain by pinching his nipple and pressing the earlobe, I get his to open the eyes. After telling me how many pills he has taken, I order an aggressive and very unpleasant treatment for the patient, it is what he deserves. I give him a brief lecture with reluctance, knowing that it will not work, most of these patients try again until they succeed, I have already done my part. I refer him to the specialist and go to my office where I have more patients waiting.

The best moment of the day arrives, the relief, I detail to my partner the details of the night, the treatments of the patients I have admitted and the tests pending review. We chatted for a while before I went to the hospital cafeteria to have a good breakfast. I'm meeting my neighbor Anthony, an Rx technician, to go home. I'll invite him, but it's better than waiting for the bus. After the revitalizer we go to the parking lot of the employees' area that is under construction.

I'm having a few days off, even though I haven't made any plans, the first thing is to sleep and rest all morning. The sun dazzles my tired eyes, thank goodness I'm wearing my expensive sunglasses. We have taken a detour to avoid the ditches and we are already approaching its modest utility, when suddenly, a blinding and powerful light invades everything, forcing us to stop abruptly, close our eyes instinctively and cover ourselves with our hands to try to protect ourselves. The sensation is very unpleasant and annoying, it's similar to being shot suddenly and without waiting by thousands of cameras with their powerful flashes, and the burst of light leaves a photonic trace on my retina that takes more than half an hour to begin to dissipate.

I have damaged my eyes, I can't open them so I can't see anything, I call Anthony who stays by my side and tells me about his situation, it's worse than mine since he wasn't wearing sunglasses. We shake hands and grope each other on a curb in the shade and wait patiently. With the area under construction, it's crazy to risk moving with everything full of ditches.

It's getting boring of so much waiting, we have been here for hours and nobody passes, I am very sleepy, we will have to start projecting another plan. While we are deciding how to act, destiny sends us help, I hear steps and a metallic background, what a relief, and finally someone is coming. I explain to him that we have become blind after the great flash, we need to be taken to the emergency room, to be attended by an ophthalmologist. He tells us that he has a motorbike and will take us one at a time. I get on first, I notice the ups and downs and the zigzag, and it gives me a feeling of insecurity so I hold on tightly for fear of falling. We are taking too long, although I remember a phenomenon, whereby time seems to pass more slowly with my eyes closed than with them open. But no, even so we have taken too long to reach the emergency room, when I get off the bike I hear people shouting for help and I ask what is happening. He answers that we are not safe there, there is danger, he would explain everything to me later, and we have to get out of there immediately. That noise was abnormal and scared me, so I let myself go. We got into an elevator and went up to one floor. Then, I sit down on a sofa, I am very thirsty after the hot morning I have endured and I ask for a glass of water.

Rapha, who is my savior's name, explains to me that most people have lost their sight. No public service works, no emergency services, everything is a chaos, a disaster and to top it off most of the people who are not affected instead of helping, are dedicated to looting, mugging and killing, that's why he has moved me to his home, a safer place. He tells me that because he was sleeping when the phenomenon happened, so he is not affected. He asks me to wait for him there, while he goes to pick up Anthony, which is fine with me. When he leaves, I lie down for a moment on the sofa, I am so tired that I fall into a deep sleep without realizing it.

I wake up startled and Rapha's warm voice calms me down, he has a deep voice, he reminds me of a film actor or radio or commercial announcer, he transmits peace and security. From his vocabulary we can deduce that he is a cultured and educated person. I immediately ask about Anthony while fearing the worst. Rapha doesn't answer me, I insist, until he tells me that he has found him inside a ditch, with his head split open by a strong blow. Surely, he must have tried to reach the emergency room by his own means, impatient for the wait. I feel sorry for him, although my relationship with Anthony was not very close, he was a good person and did not deserve that end.

Rapha cooks something fast for both of us, at dessert we exchange opinions about the new situation, about what would be the best strategy. We decided that I should stay at home, since in this state I am more of a hindrance than a help. Rapha will go out to bring food and as the situation evolves in the next few days, so we agreed.

I tell him that I need some things from the pharmacy, my periods are very irregular and painful, so to control them I take birth control pills and I have very few left in my bag. I also force him to write down a series of ophthalmological ointments and eye drops, I must start an urgent treatment for my eyes.

When I finished medicine, I decided to take my IMR, the specialty I liked best was ophthalmology but I didn't get the passing mark and in the end I had to choose the emergency specialty. Although I have always had this interest in the eye and its diseases. From the news and the data we have, it is most likely that we have been blinded by the effects of a solar flare. Our symptoms can be caused by several possibilities or a combination of them. The Sun emits electromagnetic radiation and one of them is ultra-violet rays which of course we cannot see. Intense exposure to these rays can cause keratitis, depending on the time and intensity of exposure such keratitis can be superficial or deep and affect the cornea. This produces a sensation of having a foreign body on the surface of the eye, such as grit and intense eye pain, redness of the eye, tearing and photophobia. On more serious occasions, it can cause decreased visual acuity, including temporary or permanent vision loss. These are typical injuries for welders who do not wear protection, and often occur to skiers on snow when they do not wear sunglasses. They can also affect the conjunctiva or lens, making it opaque and causing cataracts. Or affect the retina, causing the typical "burn" of the photoreceptors, this occurs, for example, by seeing a solar eclipse without adequate protection. There are also studies that assure that there is a relation between solar radiation and macular degeneration, very typical of desert places, of which this Andalusian province is proud, although I would advise everyone to use good sunglasses intensively.

I spend most of my time sitting on the couch or lying on the bed. I get really bored, I can't pass time reading or watching TV, and most of the channels don't work. My only distraction is thinking or chatting with someone, I spend hours waiting for Rapha.

I can't wait for him to arrive to start my treatment, I must try to fight against this blindness. As an affected person and as a doctor, I hope to recover my vision, I have quite a lot of knowledge about ophthalmology. Here it is, I ask Rapha to read to me very slowly the instructions for the eye drops and ointments, as well as the pills, especially the dosage. I tell him to give me a few drops of each of the eye drops, he does it clumsily, and I hope that with practice he will improve as a nurse. I need you to prepare some gauze and put in them a little of each ointment and then perform an ocular occlusion to each of my eyes. That's it, at least every twelve hours.

The days go by somewhat slowly and monotonously until he explains to me with emotion and intensity that he has saved two other girls. One in the supermarket and the other a neighbor in the building, in the attic, which because it is more spacious, the ideal for everyone is to move there. I think it's great, more company to chat with and make the hours more enjoyable. I like Rapha more and more, he's a determined guy, a real man, with his feet firmly on the ground, and he's becoming our particular hero. After the respective introductions, and while Rapha prepares dinner, we exchange our experiences of the last few days, each one telling his story with great vehemence.

How difficult and different it is to relate only by ear, without a visual perception, you don't know if the others are tall or short, thin or thick, if they are beautiful or not. Their way of dressing, their non-verbal language, in this situation you only have clues in the intonation, in the way they express themselves, in the vocabulary they use. You begin to visualize with your imagination a fictitious image of other people. Perhaps you evoke a memory of someone, because of their tone or accent, and without realizing it, you classify it and relate it to your listener. For example, Rapha has a wonderful voice, for his cadence and diction, I like to have long conversations with him. He is passionate about literature, his library must be huge, and something else we agree on, because I also love reading. Another thing in common is our love of cinema, no wonder, since most films drink from the source of good novels. Your musical tastes and mine are very similar. He has promised to rescue and check my computer to enable the special functions for the visually impaired.

I imagine him handsome and attractive, I find him very interesting, his way of behaving, always very attentive, very patient. The way he takes care of us, always looking after everything, I don't know what would happen to us without him.

But how difficult and complicated is the new life of a blind one.

As the group of blind people has increased, we need more medicine, so I ask Rapha again to make another trip to the pharmacy and get us more ointments, eye drops and pills.

After the evening, Susan and Elizabeth have retired to their respective bedrooms to rest. I look for Rapha's company, but I cannot find him. I hear moans in Susan's room, the truth is that I feel very hurt, I was beginning to be a little interested in Rapha and this fact displeases me extremely.

At mid-morning Rapha appears, very diligent, with all the medicines. We proceed to carry out the cures, as Rapha already had experience it was a more agile process and without problems, although multiplied by three. At the end he makes fun of us, as we must have got a grotesque-looking.

I should go to the hospital, maybe there is someone in the ophthalmology area, working conscientiously on the case, and I could be more helpful there. Here I just waste my time in endless waiting. Rapha has flatly refused, he tells me that the streets are still not safe and he doesn't want to take any risks, he asks me for more time and promises to take me further.

A few days have gone by, tedious ones at that, plus these girls are very scandalous, their moans never cease to echo in their rooms. It seems that here the boredom overcomes it in the bed, the Rapha this is becoming hornier and hornier. I have been quite disappointed, they have left me a little bit aside, and I don't mean that I want to be carried along by his schemes because I am a traditional girl. My ideal is to find a boyfriend for life and I give a lot of importance to loyalty. Although I'm very respectful of other people's choices and decisions, I don't judge them either, and while I search for the suitable father of my children, I take advantage of being single as much as I can for have sex.

I ask Rapha about the girls and he describes them to me physically. From what he tells me they are not of his taste, he surprises me and at the same time causes perplexity. The truth is, Rapha is taking too much advantage of the situation bearing in mind he does not like their appearances, that's why I dared to think he is lying to me or simply this guy does not care. But then he reveals something surprising, which I did not expect, it turns out that the girls are having an affair with each other, they have become very close "friends". During all these days, Rapha was alien to the wild parties that were thrown at home, which gave me an immense joy and my interest in him has reborn.

Today, lunch was abundant and exquisite, with a good wine, which makes me feel a little bit more at ease, because Rapha's cooking skills are awesome and it makes him look like a complete man!

It's a bit hot, I hear the girls panting and shouting all the time. I'm not a repressed goody two-shoes, I'm sexually active, I also have needs and I think it's my turn. I need it at least once a month, I need to let off steam and release tension. Rapha has been very good to me and I know that there is no sentimental relationship with the others, Susan has confirmed it to me. They're having fun, why not me? He's taking a nap now. I can pay him a visit and give a sweet wake-up call, it would be a way of thanking her for all he has done for me. I open the door quietly, I'll try not to let the others know. I take off my shirt and pull down my panties, I don't know if he heard me, I don't know if he's asleep or looking at me. Then, I grope my way up to the bed and straddle him, I notice that he has no shirt, his back is bare and warm, and I gently brush my nipples with his breast for a while, enjoying these caresses. He is soft, reminds me of a teddy bear, he has woken up because I feel how he massages my buttocks. He doesn't say anything, neither do I. I move my hips with cadence, soft at first, increasing the rhythm progressively until a wave of pleasure possesses me and without being able to avoid it, hungry for wet kisses, my mouth pounces on his...

Silently, quietly, I unplug myself, and somewhat shy, I go to the bathroom to spruce me up. I leave him lying there, panting, sweating, and silent. I take a long, refreshing shower.

When I go out to the living room, Susan and Elizabeth tell me that Rapha has gone out, they don't know where he is going, or how long he will be back.

We didn't hear from him again, or he had an accident or was hunted by gangs, but something bad has surely happened to him. He would never abandon us, and even less so after our intimate encounter.

The thing is, he never came back and I miss him. I'm a little sad and sorry.

We've been able to get by on our own and we understand that maybe Rapha won't take care of us anymore. The provisions will soon start to diminish, we have to look for solutions. After discussing our situation we decided to place the small portable CD player on the terrace, night and day, at full volume the repertoire of the well-known David Bowie sounds with the hope that someone will come to our aid. We run the risk of catching the attention of the bands, but our situation in a few days will be unsustainable, so we have to take the risk.

In the meantime, in spite of not observing any improvement day by day, I insist on my ocular occlusion treatment. I do not despair and today, when I changed the bandage and washed my eyes, with great effort I managed to keep them a little open, I perceived a dim light, glimpsing almost recognizable silhouettes in my room. A big smile invades my face, a nervous tingling of joy and hope runs through my being.

THE END

You can continue reading episodes of The Blind Ones by purchasing both paper and eBook at

Blog Cegados por los Libros

Roberto (Free):

https://www.smashwords.com/books/view/835734

The Blind Ones Part II:

https://www.smashwords.com/books/view/836692

About the author: Fransánchez

Fransánchez, born in 1966 in Almería He is married, with a son and a daughter to support. During his life he has worked in different tasks and companies. He lived for several years on the blessed island of Tenerife. At present he lives and works in Almería. He is very fond of cinema, series and computers. Tenacious and obstinate self-taught. Hardened reader who dares to go to the other side with his first novels and stories.

mailto:fransanchez6@hotmail.com

Blog: Cegados por los libros

Twitter: http://twitter.com/AutorCegados

Facebook: https://www.facebook.com/novela.cegados

Smashwords: https://www.smashwords.com/profile/view/Fransanchez

Amazon:https://www.amazon.com/-/es/Frans%25C3%25A1nchez/e/B01MRBJK6R

Goodreads: https://www.goodreads.com/author/show/15902902.Frans_nchez

Your Review and Word-of-Mouth Recommendations Will Make a Difference

Reviews and word-of-mouth recommendations are crucial for any author to succeed. If you enjoyed this book, please leave a review, even if it is only a line or two, and tell your friends about it. It will help the author bring you new books and allow others to also enjoy the book.

Your support is greatly appreciated!